By Charlotte Bishop

Chapter One

The term "her heart exploded within her chest" doesn't need to be so literal.

I'm standing over a body, which I do far too often, while my partner pokes, prods and tries to figure out what happened to the girl. She's lying on burgundy carpet in a convention center elevator hallway, which is done up in brass and artificial plants. Her big wig has fallen off and her Victorian era dress is crumpled up in a sad pile around her. The low-cut neckline reveals a mass of red, black and purple bruising welling up over her chest. I kill things for a living, but the bruising makes me squickier than gore does for some reason. Mostly because I can't see the pulped masses of her internal organs, so I have to imagine it.

Lionel and I are Slewfeet. Private paranormal investigators who take on cases too weird for the normal police. Human ourselves, trained to handle ghosts and monsters when they do things they shouldn't. Like this.

"Her demise must have been caused by the ire of a vengeful spirit. Thoughts?" Lionel sits up on his heels and adjusts his spectacles on his slightly pointy nose. He's a lot taller than my 5' 11", but I take spiteful satisfaction in the fact that his longish brown hair already has a few grey hairs. Mine, worn short, is purely dark blonde and going strong. Take that, thirties.

"You're the one who knows this stuff," I complain, pulling at my tight collar. To gain entry to this building without arousing suspicion, we had to dress as English lords. We're both wearing long brown frock coats with green and gold trim, knee-length breeches, and little black shoes that hurt my feet. I feel like an idiot. Lionel probably feels pretty. Why did we have to show up on the night of the Royalty Masquerade Ball? Why does anyone want to show up at a Royalty Masquerade Ball?

Dammit, our client was sure that the girl would die later tonight. He was wrong.

"I shall retire for research!" Lionel crows, throwing up his hands happily as he stands. I roll my eyes and head for the door.

"Time for a pint," I mutter, but I know I'm not getting off that easily.

"Patrick. No. There is a dead girl here," Lionel admonishes me.

"I'll have a pint while you research. What are you looking for, the ghost of someone who died of a heart attack or something? Simple enough." I loosen my collar as soon as we're away from the horde of ladies besmocked in poofy gowns and sporting white powdery faces. Sweet relief.

"If I believed there was any time to waste, we would waste it here, at this lovely ball," Lionel insists. "Sadly, we do not. So move yourself on past the pub and to the hotel."

I grumble the entire walk, of course. I have yet to understand why anyone would wear shoes like this. The one good thing about getting back to the hotel room is that I can throw these clothes on the bed and pull on a t-shirt and pajama pants.

"Do be careful with these, Patrick! They were loaned to us, not donated," Lionel scolds, smoothing out the coat with his hands. Our hotel is a very old and old-fashioned building, so all of our furniture and décor looks like it came from an antique shop. The room is painted a weird teal color and the huge, metal-framed mirror over the fireplace is so intricate I'm surprised it doesn't just break from the weight. At least the TV and kitchen appliances are from this century.

"Yeah, they're loaners from someone who can afford to have them dry-cleaned," I snap back. I dig around the mini-fridge for something to drink. I find beer. Thank whoever's up there that someone remembered to go shopping. Lionel frowns but doesn't say anything.

"Our client will have Slewfoot Headquarters deduct the cost out of your paycheck if your heavy-handedness damages these costumes."

"Oh, no he won't. That girl is dead because his information was wrong." I flop into an armchair, which creaks menacingly, and twist off the top of my beer.

Lionel's hands still. "Patrick."

"I don't know if we could have saved her. You can't deny that she would have had more of a chance of survival if we'd been there."

Lionel's lips harden into a thin line. I see the pain in his eyes.

I sigh. "Sorry. You know what I mean."

"Yes." Lionel picks up his clothes and goes into the bathroom to change. I hear the shower start up. I lean back to wait. After he's clean he'll open the laptop, and research is Lionel's area of expertise.

The reason our partnership works so well is because we acknowledge each others' strengths. Lionel teases me about him being the "brains" and me being the "brawn," but he's not far off. I'm better at swinging a weapon around and taking care of whatever we happen to be hunting. Lionel couldn't hit the broad side of a barn with a baseball bat.

Lionel comes out of the bathroom wearing a tank top and pajama pants. Oh, good, we're in for the evening. Unless something happens, of course.

"All right. Pass me a brew, would you, please?" he asks as he opens up his laptop. I'm not surprised that he wants alcohol—he pretends to disapprove of my drinking, but he enjoys a good brewski. I open one for him and sit next to him on the ancient loveseat.

The venue where we found the girl is barely twenty years old, it turns out, and there haven't been any deaths there so far. Lionel frowns and digs deeper to no avail. No one even got hurt during construction.

"Curious," he mutters. He looks up our victim's name next. The news story about her death is already up and claiming "cause of death still unknown."

"They'll say it's a heart attack, even with the...whatever...affecting all of her vital organs," I note.

"I'd imagine so, unless..." Lionel types in a few more words. "Bingo."

I lean forward and see what he's looking at. He'd searched, literally, for "Angie Collins organs explode," and lo and behold: there's an article.

"The KC Paranormal News was on the scene immediately after Angie Collins' unfortunate demise. As suspected, her organs all ruptured at the same time, identical to Harold Cunningham and Kellan Peyotr. (link)."

The link brings up another news story, posted two minutes before Angie's, on the deaths of two best friends out on a boat in the middle of a small lake.

"No spirit could have caused that pair of deaths," Lionel points out. "Water."

"Unless it was the spirit of a drowning victim."

"Those types of spirits have a tendency to follow the method of their own demise rather than develop another modus operandi."

"I don't think angry ghosts have a typical M.O."

"This reporter suspects that the police will find that all three victims died at the same moment. Evidence to support this theory is taken from an incident in the year 2003 where Ford Limon, Patricia Harvey, Manny Hintz and Holly Wrightman all died of an organ rupture at the same moment (link) while in different parts of town. Previous to that, in 1997, Ronald Simmons and Lynda Stratt died of the same phenomenon (link)."

Sure enough, there are two stories about those unfortunates. I take a healthy swig of beer.

Lionel voices my panic. "It could quite literally be anyone who has ever died of an ailment that affected the organs in this town in the past three decades."

"Welp, case closed because it's impossible to solve."

"Perhaps if I research the victims..."

"You think nine people will have some common denominator that you can find?" I ask incredulously.

"We shall have to visit the local police station. I'm sure our client can get us in or at least obtain the records we require. We will also need to go to the hospital and check any records--"

The phone rings. It's our client. Lionel puts him on speakerphone.

"You idiot son of a bitch," I begin, but the bastard cuts over me.

"Yes, regrettable, but I will mourn later. Now, *Lionel,*" he says pointedly, "How can I assist you in your search?"

"We will require access to the police and hospital records of the people whose names I will send you via email. All due respect, Mr. Jameson, I do think Patrick has a right to read you the riot act," Lionel answers, sounding apologetic. There's a sigh over the speaker.

"Fine."

"Thank you. Ahem. You idiot son of a bitch. Your information was totally wrong and Angie Collins is dead. So are two guys you didn't even mention and it's pretty obvious that the same thing killed them. You definitely didn't mention the other six people who died from this over the past couple of decades. How did you even know this was going to happen if you didn't have the details? Or did you just forget about those guys 'cause they weren't pretty? What?" I take another swig of my beer.

"I did not know who the other victims would be, or whether there would be any more. I honestly believed Angie was the only target, and that she would be the only one to die in this manner. If I had acquired any more information, I would have given it to you. As for her time of death, I had it on clearly unreliable sources." Jameson's voice is testy.

He works for someone very important or something and wants us to know it. He doesn't tolerate me very well. Cry me a river.

"All right," Lionel says quickly before I can respond. "Are there any other leads we should be following?"

"If I find something, I will call again." Jameson hangs up with that. I fight the urge to throw the phone across the room and settle for getting another beer.

"While we wait for him to fetch the paperwork, we can begin with the KC Paranormal News reporter who posted these stories," Lionel starts tapping away. "I'm certain that I can discover her name without much toil."

"Right, she's not going to be creeped out by a couple of guys showing up at her door after finding her online by breaking through her anonymous screenname."

"Malani Abdul. Age 23, senior at the local college," Lionel says as though I hadn't
spoken.

"Oh, good. Do you also have her dental records and maybe some nudies?"

Lionel shoots me a withering glare.

"We'll pay her a visit in the morning. She lives off-campus, fortunately."

"Fortunately so that she doesn't call the cops when she finds out how we found her."

"Finish your beer and go to sleep."

***

I don't really sleep well and Lionel knows it. At 2 AM, I'm still laying on my bed staring at the ceiling while he's snoring softly in the other bed. The image of Angie, lying on her back with her eyes open and her bruised chest, keeps flashing across my eyelids. I do this job because I'm good at it and because it helps people, but there are some things that always get me. I know I can't save everyone. But when we're too late—and someone almost always has to die for a client to realize there's an issue—it burns me.

Sighing, I get out of bed and go into the living room. Maybe some bad TV will put me to sleep. I've just flopped onto the loveseat (creak) and flipped on some terrible old movie when I feel eyes on me. The little hairs at the back of my neck prickle and I slowly turn my head, searching for the spy.

He's on the windowsill outside. At least, I think he's a he. Hard to tell on cats, especially when they're that fat and fluffy. He's an orange tabby cat with a peculiar pudgy face, like it gained fat like the rest of him but had to grow around his snout.

"Really, Patrick?" I mutter to myself, and turn back to the TV.

The cat is still there when I go back to bed three hours later, but he's gone when the alarm goes off at 7. Lionel is already up and bustling about. I, on the other hand, throw the clock on his bed and roll over.

"Come, Patrick, no time for sleeping in. Malani begins attending her classes in two hours."

"You got her class schedule? Creeper." I pull the covers over my head. Two hours is a nap.

"Would you rather I go by myself?" Lionel asks sympathetically. I groan.

"No. Let me shower."

Lionel has coffee made by the time I'm done in the bathroom, but as we drive over to Malani's, I'm still not seeing much besides blurs. Lionel hands me a fake police badge that says my name is Det. Louis Holloway.

"I don't look like a Louis," I mutter, but I follow him up the sidewalk anyway. The one-story house is painted with peeling light pink, though the white trim has been touched up recently. The building is surrounded by almost-exact replicas of itself in different colors.

"Typical student housing," Lionel says, nodding.

"Joy. She probably has a hulking male football star roommate who will flatten us if she freaks out," I grumble, eying the front door balefully.

"Nonsense." Lionel knocks on the door. A girl opens it. She's got a round face and dark curly hair pulled back in a headband. She's wearing a little white skirt and a blue sweatshirt that reads "Property of the Arts Dept.". Around her neck, a tiny golden heart locket no bigger than a pinky nail glimmers.

"Hi!" she chirps. I close my eyes. It's too early for chirping.

"Ms. Abdul?" Lionel asks. She nods, beaming at us. Lionel takes out his badge. "Detective Harper."

Her smile doesn't fade. "Am I in trouble?"

"No, no, my partner Detective Holloway and I just happened to come across your article on Miss Angie Collins and thought we'd ask you a few questions."

"Should you be in trouble?" I ask gruffly. Playing bad cop is all that's going to get me through this. Lionel is probably resisting the urge to step on my foot to shut me up.

"I, uh, probably shouldn't have been on the scene," Malani admits.

"Probably not," Lionel agrees, "but since you were present, we may as well attempt to use what you gleaned from your observation of the victim."

"You mean, you don't think it was a heart attack?" Malani asks. She still hasn't moved to let us in.

"Would we be here if we did, little girl? Scoot so we can come in," I snap. Malani flinches and moves back, allowing us to come into the house.

It's a mess, which might have accounted for her reluctance to let us in. Her hangdog look confirms this. There's laundry flung around everywhere and unidentifiable stains on the off-white carpet. Lionel gingerly moves some shirts aside to make room for us on the leather couch.

"Do you want anything to drink? We have soda and coffee." Malani forces a smile through her blushing.

"No, thank you," Lionel says before I can request caffeine. "Let's begin. I'm sure you have places to be."

"Right!" She hops onto the pile of laundry in an armchair and tucks her legs under her. Even in my early-morning- haze, I notice that she's got nice legs. Dark and smooth, like coffee with milk. Mmm, coffee.

Lionel pulls out a little notepad and poises a pen over the paper.

"You claim in your article that Angie Collins, Harold Cunningham and Kellan Peyotr are all dead due to the same thing, yes? How did you know about the two men?"

"I got a couple of my friends to go watch them! Do you need their names too?"

"Yes, but in a minute. How did you know to be watching these three?"

I see a little flicker of hesitation. She doesn't want to get in trouble. When she speaks, it's in hesitant little sentences.

"Well, we all take a class at school. On urban legends and myths. Lately we've been learning about, um, magic. And, well, she was teaching about some death rituals and we just kind of got caught up. Kellan, Harry and Angie were all in it too."

"Could I also have the name of your professor?" Lionel asks. His voice is kind, but Malani doesn't relax. I change my theory—it's not herself that she's worried about.

"She's not going to get in trouble, is she?"

"For simply teaching a class about magic? Heavens, no. We'd just like to talk to her. The circumstances here are, as you know, very odd indeed. We're simply trying to cover all of the bases, Miss Abdul."

"She's really cool! And if you don't have to just question her about the deaths, and you think it really is magic, she can totally help you out with it! She knows everything about magic," Malani says excitedly. Kids. Good grief.

"I'm sure. So do you, Miss Abdul, believe that these deaths were executed with magic?" Lionel makes sure to keep his face neutral.

Malani nods fervently. "Yes!"

"Does your professor?"

"I don't know if she's heard about the new ones yet, but she will. I mean, it is sort of weird, isn't it? You can't say this isn't strange."

"You didn't really answer the earlier question, though," I point out. "How did you know to be watching those particular three?"

Malani blinks at me. "Because they were using magic. Sorry, I thought I'd already mentioned it."

Chapter Two

We get the names of Malani's cohorts and teacher and then leave with a promise to come back if we had more questions. When we step outside, I spot a familiar orange face.

The cat from our window is sitting in the next door neighbor's yard.

"Hey, Garfield. Fancy seeing you here," I call to him. He meows at me and stretches out on his belly.

"Have you made that cat's acquaintance recently?" Lionel asks, surprised. I don't dislike animals, but I'm not usually very interested in them.

"He was hanging out in our window last night. I recognize his face."

"Hmmm." Lionel seems a little perturbed by the coincidence, but until I see more, I'm going to assume that he belongs to a student and leave it at that.

Lionel drives through a burger joint to get me more coffee and some breakfast.

"Your thoughts on Malani?" he asks as we head back to the hotel.

"Yor duhparmen," I gurgle around a mouthful of breakfast burrito.

"Do stop selling yourself short, Patrick. You surely made some observations that were not about her legs."

Damn, he noticed. I swallow my bite and refuse to look sheepish.

"She's a cute little cheerleader type who wound up in arts instead of business management. She's a mommy or daddy's girl, judging by her little heart necklace, which explains her absolute panic about getting in trouble."

"Couldn't the heart be from a lover?" Lionel asks.

"Too small. It's one of those keepsakes that you get when you're a baby. She's kept wearing it all these years. Seems pretty likely from that that she's also an only child and pretty spoiled."

"Anything else?"

"She's got great legs."

Lionel rolls his eyes but doesn't comment on that. "She certainly does not fit the stereotype of those who believe in magic."

"Are you kidding? Adorable little thing like that has been raised believing unicorns are real."

"Unicorns are real."

"You know what I mean."

"Outside of herself, she said that she had seen Angie, Harold and Kellan together whenever they were in the same general vicinity. All of them had a tendency to wear dark clothing, pierced body parts and pentagrams in various locations on their persons. She had spotted burns on Kellan's hands and when she inquired as to where he'd gotten them, he revealed to her that he had been participating in a ritual."

"The burns'll be on the police report."

Lionel nodded. "The next step is to find some information on this Cecily Hawthorne."

I finish my burrito. "You think the teacher might be our murderer?"

"Perhaps. She certainly knows more about these magical processes than a regular civilian should, but jumping to conclusions would hardly be in our best interests."

I lean back in my seat. Magic isn't something we have, well, any experience with and I'm not sure how much my ability to swing a crowbar or throw a punch is going to help. If we go to this Cecily Hawthorne's house and she decides to blow up our organs, that's probably it for us. I share this encouraging tidbit with Lionel.

"I harbor solid doubt that she would murder us with the precise exact spell. If the police found our bodies afterward, it would create even more suspicion," he answers. I'm not reassured.

Once we're back in the hotel room, Lionel is on his laptop looking for Cecily. He finds her class schedule and home address, as well as some personal information.

"She has inhabited a house here in the city for fifteen years and has been teaching for eight. It appears that she teaches English as well as mythology." He shows me her picture on the staff page of the college's website. She's got mid-length brown hair and green eyes; her features are pale, small, and classically pretty but not standout beautiful. She also looks way too young to have lived anywhere independently for fifteen years, but that can be deceiving.

"Her final class of the day concludes at 4, so why don't we pay her a visit after she's been in a relaxed state in her home for a time? That sort of consideration will perhaps paint us in a good light in her eyes." Lionel writes down her address and closes his computer. "For now, let us go speak with these other students."

As we leave, I think I hear the scratch of claws on the outside wall of our room. When I look, though, there's nothing.

***

The other two kids, one guy and one girl with one brain cell between them, we find in the school library trying to pass basic math. It turns out they had just been watching Cunningham and Peyotr as a favor to Malani.

"I don't believe in that crap," Marcus says, shaking his head. He's big and Mexican, wearing a letter jacket. "I just want to get Malani in the--"

"Lovely, thank you," Lionel interrupts, turning to the blonde girl, Natalie. "And you?"

"Malani and I have been friends for, like, a semester. That's long enough to be doing stupid, weird things for her, right?"

"And you don't find the deaths strange? I mean, that's what you witnessed. Simultaneous death," I try.

"I mean, yeah, but they just had heart attacks. The police said so." Natalie nods earnestly.

"Was a little creepy, though," Marcus admits. "They just start screaming and twitching, right, and we called 9-1-1 but it was too late."

I shudder minutely. "If you guys thought there were going to be deaths, why didn't you call before?"

"What would I say? 'Hey, cop, I'm trying to sleep with this girl and she asked me to watch these guys to see if they die, so could you come out in case their hearts explode?'"

"Point," Lionel says dryly.

"No point. If you call the police about death, they'll come," I say. Marcus flinches and looks at his lap.

"Look, Detective, we were just doing what Malani asked us to do, okay? What's done is done." Natalie glares at me. I match it.

"People are dead."

"Heart attacks aren't our fault!"

"Children," Lionel grits out. His eyes fix on me. "This is not an argument regarding ethics. This is a police investigation."

"Fine. So you're both in Cecily Hawthorne's class, right?" I ask, grinding my teeth.

"Yeah. Sounded like an easy A. It isn't, but it sounded like one." Marcus looks morose.

"She was talking about rituals and stuff for killing people," Natalie supplies. "The organ-explodey one was the one that kinda stood out."

"Let us hypothetically assume that you do believe in magic. Does Ms. Hawthorne seem to you to be the sort of person to murder others using ritual spells?" Lionel asks.

"She's a crazy cat lady, so yeah." Natalie nods.

"Psh, no. She's hot and nerdy," Marcus says.

We're not going to get any help here on that front. I sigh and stand up.

"We'll be in touch," Lionel says. I'm so frustrated that I'm having to resist the urge to tear my hair out by the time we get outside.

"We forgot to ask Malani why she didn't call anyone," I point out.

"Most likely for the same reason as Marcus, Patrick. These are children, infants in the ways of the world. Besides, you and I know full well that the police would have been of no help whatsoever. Malani at least is intelligent enough to be aware of that as well."

"Yeah, but what if that Marcus kid saw a mugging?"

"It is not our job to parent them. It is our job to solve this despicable case and bring a murderer to justice." Lionel sighs. I hate upsetting him, so I let it go by looking away. As I do, I spot an orange tail flicking around the corner of a building. My eyes narrow, but I mean, it's a cat. I guess he just likes me.

We get some lunch and call Jameson.

"Magic? That seems a tad farfetched." Jameson sniffs. Asshole.

"More farfetched than ghosts?" I'm incredulous.

"Well, yes. There's a logical explanation for ghosts. Unfinished business and all that. I think you should still be looking for the angry dead."

"If our visit to the victims' professor yields no fruit, we shall return posthaste to our previous theory," Lionel says.

"Very well. The police and hospital records have been delivered to your room. I hope they prove useful." Jameson hangs up without a goodbye. That guy really grinds my gears.

We spend the afternoon poring over the records. The oldest, the ones from 1997, explain it away as "extremely severe" heart attacks for the victims regardless of the fact that both were young, healthy and had no history of health problems. In fact, neither did the next three. Coroners looked for poison first and eventually had to put it down as a heart attack.

None of the victims had ever even had a cold, and none of them had allergies of any kind. All of them were the healthiest cadavers any of the coroners had ever seen in their entire careers. They'd all just simply dropped dead of severe heart attacks that had ruptured their other organs as well.

Less of a heart attack and more of a "body attack," said one report.

"Something is really weird," I say, frowning. Lionel nods, looking troubled as well.

"That's the common denominator, certainly, other than all victims residing here in the city. I fear that this predicament is present on a larger scale even than we surmised. It seems we will be required to thoroughly investigate the victims to find their murderer."

"Or murderers," I point out. "Cecily hasn't been here for all of these killings."

"We shall be forced to convince Jameson's connections to inquire as to whether Ms. Hawthorne was perhaps present in town for a visit in 1997 to be certain, but you raise a good point. You see? I have told you on many occasions that your powers of deduction are plenty adequate."

I snort. Lionel ignores it.

"The current modus operandi is that only one set of victims dies at a time, so perhaps time is on our side. However, we must solve this before the killer discovers our true identities and involvement." He chews his bottom lip the way he always does when he's nervous.

"Is it possible that they killed themselves? Maybe they were trying to perform this ritual on somebody else and it backfired," I suggest.

"Only Harold and Kellan were together at the time. If their purpose was to eliminate poor Angie, though, perhaps it was successful in part but also fatal to the two boys." Lionel scribbles it down. "We'll check on that angle also."

I glance at the clock. "Cecily will be home by now."

"Ah, yes. We'd better go see her."

***

Cecily Hawthorne's house is small but nice. Fairly modern with two stories and wood paneling. The whole thing is painted in browns and whites. The screen door has one of those elaborate black metal coverings with leaves and curves, which looks slightly out-of-place on a typical porch. The welcome mat says "Dogs Live Here, So Stay Out Of My Stuff." Must be little dogs because the doggie door is only a foot high.

"She sounds friendly," I say to Lionel, pointing at the mat. He clears his throat and rings the bell. With the sun going down, it's getting a little chilly, so I'm wearing my windbreaker and he's wearing a light trench coat. I draw my jacket a little closer around me. There is *something* about this house. It's probably just my nerves. The doorbell elicits the barking of what sounds like a fairly good-sized dog. I arch an eyebrow at the dishonest pet door.

Cecily opens the door, her hand wrapped around the collar of a black dog that comes up to just over her knee, which puts it a little below mine. The dog's muzzle is dusted grey and its eyes are just a touch clouded. An old mutt.

Cecily is wearing glasses with trendy dark plastic frames, which wasn't in her picture. She must have been in for the night because she's sporting a men's white tank top and grey knee-length pajama bottoms. Her only jewelry is a chain around her neck, whatever's at the end disappearing into her shirt. I find her more attractive this way than I did when she was snazzied up for her staff picture on the school's website.

"Can I help you?" she asks, dragging the dog back a few more inches. "Sorry, I promise she's friendly but she'll knock you over trying to sniff you."

Lionel runs through the same spiel he gave Malani while I surreptitiously check behind Cecily into the house. All I can see is a short hallway covered in salmon-colored paint, dark brown wood trims and furniture, and a few knick-knacks on the walls. There's a doorway to her right, a stairway to her left and a brown swinging door at the end of the hall. A huge shaggy head pushes that door open and meets my eyes. One of the biggest dogs I've ever seen comes trotting out to see what all the fuss is. This one looks like a black-and-gold bear-wolf with enough fur to make several coats - I can't imagine Cecily's grooming bills for it.

"He's friendly too," Cecily says when she sees where my eyes are. "Come on in."

As though to reassure us, the big dog's tongue comes lolling out of his mouth in a happy grin. Lionel and I step inside once Cecily manages to pull the smaller one back. Cecily directs us to the living room, through the doorway to her right, and asks for permission to let the smaller dog go. The mutt comes up to me and starts checking every inch that she can reach with her nose. I sort of awkwardly pet her, but she doesn't seem to want my attention. She moves away to check Lionel as soon as she's sniffed everywhere she can on me. Her blue collar has "Lyla" sewn into it in magenta letters.

Lionel, unlike me, really likes dogs, so he squats down where she can reach his face. As she sniffs, he rubs all over her face and neck, saying things like "good girl" and "what a sweet creature." She blatantly ignores his affection and trots off as soon as she's done. However, the bigger dog has now pegged Lionel as a dog person and he comes thundering up to get his love. In fact, he actually bowls Lionel over entirely in his enthusiasm. We don't get much amusement in our job so I'm gratified to see Lionel laughing out loud at the big creature.

I sit down on the brown leather couch and look around the room. Cecily's living room has a few shelves and tables that are covered with little statues of dragons, unicorns, and, inexplicably, penguins. A few photographs hanging on the wall show her dogs and I'm guessing some of her friends or students, but she's only in a couple of them. One photo in particular catches my eye: a young man, movie-star-handsome, with Spanish features and long hair in a ponytail. Weird dye job - the hair is black to the ponytail holder and white the rest of the length. The reason it stands out is that it looks like a very old picture, faded into almost sepia tones without the aid of a phone app or Photoshop, but the guy looks pretty modern with that crazy hair.

Cecily comes back in with three beers clutched in her fingers. She hands one to me, one to Lionel, and then sits down in the armchair catty-corner to the couch. She pulls her bare feet up under her. The big dog leaves Lionel with a final lick to his face and starts following her around. He lies down on the floor in front of her chair. The older dog nestles up to him and promptly goes to sleep.

"I heard you laughing at Sas. He really loves people," Cecily starts off.

"Sas?" I ask, taking a swig of beer. It's a good, dark one. I make a mental note of the brand name.

"Sasquatch."

That makes me chuckle. I kind of like her already.

Until she meets my eyes squarely and says, "So. It's been awhile since Slewfeet have bothered me."

Chapter Three

I see Lionel's smile vanish and he sits up straighter. He hasn't touched his beer yet. I try to look nonchalant as I put mine down on the coffee table.

"I don't mind," Cecily continues. "I'm guessing it has something to do with the recent murders. I'm happy to help."

"What gave us away?" Lionel asks.

"Fake police badges and the timing. Plus, I assume you do the talking because your partner can't act his way out of a paper bag." She takes a drink from her beer.

"Hey!" I yelp.

Cecily smiles a little into her beer. "I can tell you what kind of ritual was used, but it's going to be up to you to--"

"Hold up, lady. We're here to question you," I interrupt, feeling like we've totally lost control of this situation.

"That's correct," Lionel says. "We were told you were teaching about this sort of thing in one of your classes. Rather suspicious behavior."

"If I know about Slewfeet, why would I be blatantly doing something suspicious knowing I'd get caught if I were the murderer?" Cecily shakes her head. I pick up my beer again. Hey, if she poisoned it, I'd already be dead, right?

"Well, all right. For now. What can you tell us about the ritual used?" Lionel asks.

"It's obviously witchcraft," she says, but I interrupt her again.

"As opposed to what?"

"Sorcery."

"How do you know it's witchcraft and not sorcery?"

"If it were sorcery there wouldn't be much in the way of bodies left," she explains. "It's about subtlety. Witchcraft can do things like destroy parts of the body without leaving a mess. Sorcery is, basically, kablooey magic. Therefore, since the spell involved here has to be witchcraft, it has to be ritualistic in nature."

"Witches are required to use rituals?" Lionel asks, leaning forward eagerly. We're going to be here a while. That's his "fascinated" tone of voice.

"Exactly. Sorcerers are born to magic, but witches learn it. This particular ritual is, as I'm sure you suspect, nasty. It involves rupturing a sacrificial animal's organs with a sterile, hot needle while it's still alive. Because this is a death ritual, there have to be at least three witches present or there won't be enough power."

"It takes multiple murderers to kill?"

"One sorcerer can kill someone. Witchcraft, because it has to channel via ritual, isn't as strong. They'd also need something from the victims. Hair or blood, usually. To connect with them strongly enough to kill them."

"So, the witches would have to be in a position to acquire something like that. A classmate. Or even a friend." Lionel leans back again, looking thoughtful.

"Or just a really good cat burglar," I say. "Malani said the victims were using magic, too."

"Not all of the witches in town have to be from the same coven," Cecily says. "You could be dealing with a territory war."

"A territory war induced around once per decade, perhaps." Lionel nods to himself.

"That would help explain why the attacks aren't even, like every ten years on the dot," I agree.

"Cecily, do you know who the witches around here are?"

"Kellan was the only one I was sure about, and that's only because I overheard his conversation with Malani about his burns. Angie and Harold looked more like, well, your stereotypical kids going through a phase. But I sort of figured them. Witches tend to keep to their coven and not branch out when it comes to making new friends."

"Can't ever be easy, like 'witches are green' or something," I mutter.

"Sorry. Since witches use learned magic, it doesn't affect them physically."

"Does it affect sorcerers?" I ask out of bored curiosity.

"There's always something physically off about a sorcerer, yes. Has to do with the fact that they're conceived with at least one parent under a spell."

Suddenly, Sas' huge head perks up and he stares at the door. I hear the doggie door open up.

"Ah, it's about that time. I hope you're not allergic to cats." Cecily hops over the dogs onto the floor and pads off into the hallway. Sas follows her after carefully removing himself from Lyla, who doesn't even move. I hear a chorus of meows.

"Yes, yes, it's all set up in the kitchen," Cecily is saying. I lean around to look, and the sight is pretty crazy. About seven or eight cats are coming in through the doggie door, twining around Cecily's legs as they pass her to go into the kitchen. A familiar pudgy face peers around the corner and meets my eyes.

"Ack!" I nearly fall backward. The lanternlike eyes blink languidly at me and he lets out a loud meow. Cecily picks him up and comes into the living room. Sas follows dutifully at her heels. Lionel recognizes the fat cat, too.

"Do you guys know each other?" Cecily asks as the cat's eyes continue to stare into mine.

"He's been following me all day and he was in my window last night," I say. "He's creepy!"

"Are these all your cats?" Lionel asks, obviously recalling Natalie's scorn.

"No, I just feed them. I'm pretty sure most of them belong to someone. I'm sure Jack here does. He's so chubby." Cecily frowns a little. "You said he's been following you?"

"I see him everywhere I go."

"He's not even all that friendly, much less the stalker type." Cecily sounds a little uncomfortable. She gingerly puts the cat down. He promptly heads for me. I see Sas' eyes following him, but the big dog doesn't move from his place next to Cecily.

Jack rubs his head against my legs and purrs loudly enough to vibrate my ankle. He hops into my lap and settles in. He's fast asleep in seconds.

Lionel bursts out laughing. "You've made a friend!"

I'm dumbfounded. I don't even *like* animals that much. Then again, I've heard that cats love people who don't like them. Lionel reaches out to pet Jack, but the cat hisses and lashes out. My partner pulls his hand back and pouts at the blood welling up from three shallow but long scratches.

"Cats have never been too fond of me," he says.

Cecily graciously gets both of us another beer and settles back into her chair. Sas nuzzles Lyla as he lays back down; her rheumy eyes open just enough for her to see him. Then she's out again. Cecily gives both of them a gentle scratch before getting her own beer again.

"All right. You're going to have to find the coven's base. It's most likely going to be someone's house, probably in a basement or spare room. You'll recognize it by the pentagrams and weird stuff lying around," she says, her voice dry.

"Are you going to help out?" I ask.

"I do information, but I'm not risking my life, no. I like you guys and I hope you win, rah-rah, give me an S," she pumps a fist into the air, "but witches, especially paranoid ones, are super dangerous." She glances down at Sas and Lyla, and as much as I want to be indignant, I realize that she loves them like children. I mean, to me, they're dogs and not on the same level as people. But to her they're much more. I sigh as I come to the conclusion that we can't ask her to potentially orphan them.

"Can we have a phone number for you, at least?" Lionel asks. She writes it down for him.

"What makes you think they're paranoid?" I ask her.

"I would be, now that Slewfeet are in town." She hands Lionel the slip of paper.

"How would they know?"

"Like I said. Timing."

***

I manage to get out from underneath Jack (despite his loud protests) and we say our goodbyes. I notice that Lionel makes some small talk as we go. Once we're in the car, I punch him lightly on the shoulder.

"You think she's cute!"

Lionel stiffens. "She is...cute, yes, but that's hardly--"

"You could have gotten her phone number any old way, you sly dog, but you chose to ask her for it! My little man is all grown up." I wipe an imaginary tear.

"She strikes me as an intellectual young woman with a deep-seated love for animals. She is a wealth of knowledge when it comes to the supernatural. Of course I would find her alluring as we have much in common." Lionel's language gets even more formal when he's flustered. This is adorable.

"Don't let her distract you too much until the job's finished," I mock-scold as we pull away from her house. She stands on the porch with Sas and watches us go. I wave. She sort of half-waves back and then goes into the house.

"You are incorrigible."

"Okay, Webster." I chuckle to myself all the way back to the hotel. Jameson, of course, wipes the grin from my face. It's not a phone call this time - he's sitting on our loveseat when we enter the room. He's a little beyond middle-aged and doughy. He's wearing a tailored suit and shiny shoes. Curly dark hair is slicked severely back from his face to explode in a poof towards the back, like it just refuses to obey the gel. This style shows off a badly-receding hairline. Does he look in a mirror?

"I was in the area," he says by way of greeting. "What do you have from the teacher?"

"Cecily is a Slewfoot informant, actually. So we have an ally rather than a suspect," Lionel tells him before going on to explain what she told us.

"Are you certain she's trustworthy?" Jameson asks when he's finished, his eyes narrowed.

Lionel, I can see, bites back a snarky retort. "Patrick and I still live, yes."

"Did you search her house?"

"Indeed not," Lionel says.

"Then how do you know it isn't her conducting these rituals? She couldn't have killed you on the spot if it takes a ritual to deliver the final blow. For all you know, she has your hair and is setting you up to die now. She made you trust her with, perhaps, even more magic."

"I thought you didn't believe in magic," I say to save Lionel's pride.

"This seems to be the explanation for the deaths. I have no choice." Jameson shakes his head. "I'm disappointed in you two, immediately trusting a pair of big eyes."

"What do you suggest?" Lionel grits out. I'm surprised at him, making his dislike so plain. I guess he really liked Cecily.

"I suggest that you go back and search her house."

"You mean break into the house with two dogs, one of which is big enough to kill us by stepping on us the wrong way?" I ask.

"Clearly that is her security system, which she allowed you to see so that you would be too afraid to do exactly as I am suggesting."

The worst part of all of this is that I can see Jameson's point. We did trust Cecily awfully fast, just because she mentioned Slewfeet and was willing to give us information. Information that won't do us any good if she is, in fact, the killer.

"After all, you didn't think to ask for protective spells, did you? She certainly didn't offer them." Jameson is still on a roll.

"Look, why don't YOU do the job if you're so much smarter than we are?" I snarl at him.

"Do not blame me for your lack of skill. Frankly, I am incredibly surprised at you, Lionel. I had great respect for your--"

"Don't you insult Lionel," I say. "He's so much smarter than you that it would make your head spin."

Jameson's look could wither a plant. "Coming from the barely-trained monkey, those words are hardly a shock. A dog that knows to bring back the ball would seem a genius to you. Lionel must practically be Einstein."

That's it. I'm going to punch him. Only Lionel's hand twisting into the back of my jacket keeps me from lunging at him, and to my satisfaction, Jameson rears back in his chair when he sees the look on my face.

"I said to shut your goddamn mouth."

"We will never be employed again," Lionel moans softly behind me.

"Oh, you'll work again, I'm sure." Jameson stands up and straightens his coat. "Just not for my employer. Nor for me. You will, however, search this woman's house tonight."

"Mr. Jameson--" Lionel tries.

"I said you will search her house. If you are certain that she is on the level then I'm sure she'll consent to a thorough investigation. If you're not 100 percent, however, you'll break in like the Slewfeet you are and you'll find her guilty or not."

Jameson looks down his nose at us for a moment before storming out of the room.

"Great, he can get in here whenever he wants," I mutter, yanking my jacket out of Lionel's hand and straightening it.

"Patrick, you *must* learn to control your temper." Lionel's voice is weary rather than angry.

"I didn't hit him!"

"You would have."

We spend the next hour preparing to break into Cecily's house. Lionel won't say it, but he knows the same dismal thing that I do: Jameson was right. Cecily is still a suspect.

Preparation for me is digging out my long, lightweight trench coat and checking to make sure everything I need is still in it. Pistol, check. Ammo, check. Bowie knife, check. Baton...not check.

"Dammit," I swear softly, rolling my eyes and dragging my suitcase over to the bed. My baton is at the bottom, buried under extra undies and two paperbacks. "There you are, baby."

My baton was specially made for me by a blacksmith possessed by a friendly ghost - not Casper, exactly, but close. It's about the length of my arm. Half of it is iron worked through with silver, and the other half is silver worked through with iron. Basically, it doesn't matter what kind of baddie I hit with it. Ghosts can't stand iron, vampires and werewolves don't do silver, and anything else is going to get walloped in the face by ten pounds of solid metal. By far my favorite weapon.

There's a special pocket sewn into my Slewfoot-official coat for it. I lovingly slide it in before checking on Lionel. He's got all of his equipment spread out neatly on his bed. He looks pretty upset as he methodically places each item into his various pockets.

"Hey, man, look. We won't even make a mess. In, out, she'll never know we were there." I pat his shoulder reassuringly.

"It isn't that. Not just that, rather. I do regret that we're forced to invade Cecily's privacy, but I also feel chagrined that Jameson saw what we did not. It makes me worry that perhaps Cecily did strike us with some sort of enchantment."

I know better. Lionel doesn't *get* crushes on girls very often. He's certainly never seen a suspect in that light. That makes him even more suspicious of Cecily and even angrier with himself for the lapse in judgment.

I hurt for him, and that makes me angry too. At both Cecily and Jameson. It's probably irrational, but I don't care.

"Let's go get it over with."

Chapter Four

We park a block away from her house. The neighborhood is almost completely dark at this hour. We're able to walk down the sidewalk without fear of being seen.

"How are we distracting Sasquatch and Lyla?" I ask quietly.

"We'll be forced to--"

I never learn what we'd be forced to do. Lionel's eyes suddenly shoot open wide, and he drops to the pavement with a grunt. I'm frozen for an instant. Then I see his hand clutching his chest, and I know what's happening.

"No, no, no!" I drop down next to him and try to pull him up. "Lionel, what do I do?!"

He can't talk. A spasm forces him to double up; he's in so much pain that he can't even scream. Tears stream from his eyes.

"Lionel! You have to tell me what to do!"

He rolls over on his side and curls up in the fetal position. He whimpers like a child. I want to start screaming for help, but what could anyone do? There are tears in my own eyes as I kneel there. Stunned into inactivity as I watch my best friend dying in front of me.

Suddenly I hear deep barking. Then Sasquatch is thundering along the sidewalk toward me with Cecily running behind him. Lights are turning on in the houses around us, but I'm focused on her.

"Patrick! Help me get him up!" She kneels down next to Lionel. I just stare at her. Sasquatch dances around us and licks at Lionel's hands, whimpering.

"Patrick!" Her hand cracks across my face so hard that I actually have to catch myself to keep from hitting the ground. "Now!"

Together we pull Lionel to his feet and half-drag him across the ground to Cecily's front door. She manages to get the screen door open. Sasquatch sits in front of it to hold it open. As soon as both of Lionel's feet are in the door, he takes a huge gulp of air and starts coughing. Cecily guides us to the couch, whistling for her dog who comes running into the room, letting the screen door slam closed. Lyla comes trotting in to see what the ruckus is.

I kneel next to Lionel's head. He's passed out. Deathly pale, but breathing steadily. I frown and look up at Cecily. She looks much less worried than I feel she should.

"What happened?" I snap. She arches an eyebrow at me and shows me the back of Lionel's hand. The scratches Jack gave him are literally pulsing. As I watch, the pulsing slows and stops.

"He crossed my threshold," she says. As though that explains everything, or anything at all. I stand up shakily, my fists clenching.

"That doesn't tell me anything! What did you do?!"

"Saved his life. Sas woke up, which woke me up. I heard you yelling. Bringing him through my threshold stopped the flow of the spell into his body." Cecily regards me warily. She's got her arms wrapped around herself, as though she's cold. Or scared. Or just pulling into herself.

Sas is sitting next to her. He looks up at me with his ears perked up and eyes unblinking. Not aggressive - just ready. I realize how angry I am, but I'm not angry with her. I'm angry with myself. I'm angry with my inability to save my partner.

"What is a threshold?" I ask to calm myself. I sit back down to lean against the couch.

She takes a step back. "It's a blockade that keeps spells from getting in here."

"And how," I continue, noticing her nervousness, "did you get one?"

Cecily looks at me for a long moment. I can see something working in her head. Then she drops her arms, placing one hand on Sas' huge head, and blinks.

For a second I don't see a difference. Then I guess my eyes focus on hers, because in the middle of her olive eyes is the slit pupil of a cat.

"Gah!" I stand up, fall over, and hit the back of my head on the couch's arm. I rub my head and hear her say to Sas, "See? The big reveal could have gone worse." The big dog whines softly in his throat.

My first instinct is to draw my baton and whale on her. Two things stop me: the massive animal at her side and the fact that Lionel is only alive because of her.

"Okay," she says. She turns away to bustle around the room. "I'm a sorcerer. We're past that? Good. Now. They have Lionel's blood due to Jack's scratching him, which means that if he leaves here tonight, he'll die. You might as well get comfortable."

A blanket hits me in the face, followed closely by a pillow. I'm guessing that while Cecily wasn't particularly surprised by my reaction to the revelation of her nature, she was also hurt. I don't apologize, though. Ally or not, she wasn't straightforward and she's not human. That puts her in my bad books.

"Patrick?" Lionel's voice is weak, but I'm just relieved it's there. Cecily hurries over as well. Her cat eyes are wide with worry. I don't think Lionel is really focusing yet because he stares at her with a look of total admiration.

"You *are* an ally," he whispers, and smiles. Cecily puts her hands to her mouth. To her credit, she doesn't change her eyes back, but after a pause she nods and leaves the room.

"So she's a sorcerer," I tell Lionel as the seconds of him staring after her stretch into minutes. Lyla follows her, but Sas lays down next to Lionel and goes to sleep.

"So I gathered," Lionel replies dreamily. "It's the eyes. And the fact that I still breathe."

I stare at him. "Lionel. She's not human. Stop looking like that."

The smile drops from his face as he turns his head to look at me. His exhausted eyes are troubled.

"Patrick, she saved my life. You cannot possibly be placing her in the same headspace as the murderous witches."

"Nonhuman is nonhuman. I'm not going to shoot her, but I don't trust her either." I look away. "She lied to us, Lionel."

"Because of Slewfeet, and people, like you, who abhor anyone who claims nonhuman heritage."

I'm not sure he means to say it that way, but regardless, it makes my heart clench up. I know I'm being a bigot right now, but how I feel is how I feel. My baton, pistol, and I have dealt with nonhumans for most of my life, and I'm not going to be able to change my opinion of an entire minority based on the actions of one.

"Well, now she knows that I'm not going to do anything to her," I reason. "I don't think she particularly needs me to like her."

Lionel sighs, but he lets it go. I think he's just too tired to argue. His hand falls to land lightly on Sas' head; the big dog's ears twitch, but he doesn't open his eyes. And just like that, Lionel is asleep. I put my blanket over him and lean back against the couch with my head on the pillow that Cecily gave me.

I don't sleep.

***

I hear Cecily's voice on the phone sometime before the sun is completely up. She sounds terse and a bit like she's trying to calm someone down. I get up (ow, my back) and go see what's going on. It might not be any of my business, but since Cecily doesn't strike me as the type to have a lot of friends or family, I assume it's about the case.

Cecily's kitchen is nice, with big appliances and a bar with two tall chairs. The sink is about half-full of dishes. There are more penguin knickknacks on the shelving under the window. I nearly trip over Lyla who's lying in the doorway. She looks up at me like I've offended her deepest sensibilities.

"I don't know," I hear Cecily saying. "Malani, I don't understand why you think I would know."

Her eyes, still cat-slit, flick to me, but then she turns her back. For some reason that makes my heart twinge. But only a little.

"Natalie was a sweet girl, Malani. I don't know why they would have killed her unless she got into something she shouldn--oh, Malani, you didn't. Marcus too? I told you to stay out of all of this. I'm sure they'll find Marcus' body soon. Oh, Jesus, I'm sorry, don't cry..."

Cecily climbs up onto one of the high chairs. She sets her elbow on the bar and rests her forehead on her hand. I step a little further into the room. I feel a little awkward about listening in on this conversation. Since it's related to the case, however, I don't leave.

"It isn't your fault," Cecily lies. She glances at me again.

"It is too," I mouth at her. She glares at me, which is pretty creepy coming from eyes like those.

"No, Malani. Yes, I know you're scared and you should be, but if you stay home they won't get what they need from you. Because I don't want you to. I have a very sick friend over and I'm not taking care of both of you."

"Cold," I mouth.

"You're a strong girl. Just hold on. It'll all be over soon. I promise. No, I can't tell you how I know, and I know that's not very reassuring. But I do promise. Okay. Call again if you need to." Cecily hangs up and sighs. "Natalie Carter was found dead in her dorm room this morning."

"She was the blonde cheerleader-y one, right?" I ask for clarification.

"Yeah. Marcus McKinney hasn't been seen since after his football practice yesterday, either. He's the other one you interviewed."

"We'll find out that time of death was the same time that Lionel was attacked, won't we?"

"I'd imagine so, yes."

"Natalie was a cheerleader? So in super good health, and what, 19? 20? And the police are still going to say this is some kind of heart attack?" Cover-ups always irk me, even though I know the need for secrecy. If regular humans knew about the supernatural, they'd all live in fear all the time. It would be the Spanish Inquisition all over again with genocides thrown in for good measure.

"Probably." Cecily opens up her phone again. "I need to call the school."

I leave her to her responsibilities and go back into the living room. Lionel is sitting up. His hand rests over his chest.

"Feel okay?" I ask him.

"A little sore," he says.

"Well, your organs were falling apart," Cecily says as she comes in with a steaming mug of tea for Lionel (and one for herself.)

"Where's my tea?" I demand.

"I was going to make you some, but decided against it when I remembered that your face was slightly different from my perception of what a face should look like."

Lionel chokes on his tea. I try to mimic Jameson's withering stare, but that only makes it worse. While my loyal partner tries to contain himself, Cecily curls up in her armchair with her own tea. Sas goes to lie at her feet. He pants happily as it probably appears to him that everyone is a big happy family.

I don't reply to Cecily's jab. Instead, I just let her fill Lionel in on the events of the morning.

"We'll need to examine the body. It must be determined whether or not she, too, was scratched by a cat. If there are no marks present on the body, we'll need to speak with Natalie's friends and acquaintances. Anyone close enough to her to acquire some sort of body part or fluid from her." He's in his element now.

"What about Malani? Is she a suspect here?" I ask. Both of my compatriots turn slowly to look at me like I've said something either offensive or shocking.

"What? She knew all of the victims and was close enough to Natalie to get her hair or something. She was on the scene for Angie's murder and was the first to call Cecily about Natalie. Plus, how likely is it that of the three on the scene, she's the only one who hasn't been killed or disappeared?" I cross my arms, feeling put-out that no one appears to be taking me seriously.

"Well, she is also the only one of the three who believes in this sort of thing. She'd be a touch more cautious," Lionel says.

"I have a hard time buying Malani as evil, but it wouldn't hurt to check," Cecily says. After the events of the past 10 hours or so, I'm surprised to *hear* her agreeing with me even if she does. Clearly, she's not the type to let personal grudges get in the way of the case.

"Is there something, anything, that we could be specifically looking for when it comes to Natalie's acquaintances?" Lionel asks Cecily.

"Obviously, things like burns on their hands or pentagrams somewhere on their bodies. Most of them won't be that obvious, though, and you're looking for at least three. Probably a lot more."

"You've lived here for fifteen years and have never bothered to scout out the local magical competition?" I ask, incredulous.

"Why would I? Acting like competition would just bring trouble down on my head and put anyone I got close to in danger. I can protect myself. They can't." She gestures at the photos on her wall. Her other hand buries itself in Sas' fur; he looks up at her with a soft whine.

"You're kind of a coward." The words jump out of my mouth before I can stop them, and I'm not sure I would have if I'd thought about it. Lionel opens his mouth to berate me, but Cecily just looks me in the eyes.

"I've loved and lost more than a bigot like you could comprehend," she says softly. There's deep rage and hurt in her voice, but it doesn't tremble. "Call it cowardice if you want. I don't need nor desire your opinion on how I live my life."

Sas stares at me, as though he understands what's going on. He's not tensed up, but I'm pretty sure he'd be on me in less than a second if Cecily said "sic 'im." It reminds me that, no matter how friendly he is, he loves Cecily like his mother and Lionel and I are dispensable in his world.

It also reminds me that I'm the only creature in this house who doesn't think Cecily hung the freaking moon. Irritating.

I sigh. "Fine, whatever. So is Jack a familiar or what?"

"A skilled witch can connect with a cat and use it to do his or her will, yes. Permanent familiar, probably not, but for the witch's purposes Jack did what was needed. More than likely that witch is Jack's owner, but not necessarily."

"This is getting so convoluted," I mutter.

"It's a place to start. Bonding with Jack in that manner would be easier for a person that knows him well." Cecily shrugs. "I'm just saying that a really powerful witch could do it to a strange animal."

"Do you think these are powerful witches that we're dealing with?" Lionel asks her.

"At least one of them is and more likely all three. Killing someone isn't a novice's game. Targeting five people even less so."

"Is it safe for Lionel to go anywhere?" I ask.

Cecily nods. "The power his blood had over him waned with the rising of the sun. If they try again, the blood they have won't be strong enough to do more than twinge a bit."

"We'd best get started then." Lionel stood up with a grunt. "They'll try something else sooner or later."

Chapter Five

It turns out that Natalie was friends with everyone. Of course she was.

We start with the cheerleading squad just for giggles. A lot of giggles. I leave Lionel to it about halfway through and wander off to interview the coach.

"Natalie? Sweet thing. Huge shame about what happened." The coach is a pretty woman with dark eyes, black hair tied back in a ponytail and a natural tan. Her blue track suit covers all of her, which is terrible for me because 1) I can't check her for pentagrams and 2) well, the obvious.

"Seems to me there's no way she could have had a heart attack. She was athletic and a healthy eater," I say.

"It is kind of bizarre, but I guess it really can happen to anyone."

"Don't you think it's weird that students from this school are dying from the same thing?"

She frowns at me. "What are you trying to say? This isn't a movie, guy."

Either she's the best actress in the world or she's innocent. I mold my face into the very picture of chagrined and excuse myself. I head back to Lionel. He extricates himself from the cheerleader gaggle, several of whom are crying.

"Man, you're great with women," I observe as we walk away.

"They have lost a friend and teammate, Patrick. Do have some compassion. Apparently half of them aren't even in attendance today. They're distraught."

"Or terrified because they've seen enough horror movies to know that something's going down."

"They would probably assume some sort of illness before thinking of the supernatural," Lionel says.

"Either way, we can't check them all if they're not here. Lionel, we've *got* to find a way to narrow this search down."

"I suggest that we take a detour and visit Marcus' house. Perhaps we will find some connection."

Marcus lived in a two-story house with about four other guys on the football team. Two of them are home when we walk up. We flash our fake detective badges and they're amiable to letting us check out Marcus' room.

It's not a huge shock to find that he lived in a pigsty. There's dirty laundry everywhere, take-out containers filling the trash can, and dirt all over every surface. Lionel wrinkles his nose.

"Good Lord."

That's the closest he ever comes to a swear word, so I know he's offended. I look away to hide my amused grin. Something shiny catches my eye.

"Lionel." I make my way over to Marcus' filthy desk and pick up a tiny statue from the corner. It's a woman, made of silver, draped in Greek-style clothing and holding two torches. Very stereotypically un-jock.

"Hecate," Lionel breathes. He comes to stand beside me and adjusts his glasses. "The goddess of witchcraft."

"That's not suspicious at all," I mutter, setting the statue down on the desk again.

"It appears that Marcus may not have been entirely truthful with us." Lionel opens Marcus' laptop and starts tapping away. I glance over to see that he's breaking Marcus' password. I open the closet while he's busy with that.

A wave of aroma hits me, but it isn't the nasty sweat-stench I was expecting (or at least, not completely.) There's a strong smell of herbs and incense coming from a row of shoeboxes lining the middle shelf of the closet. A quick check through them reveals little bags and jars of all kinds of dried plants. One shoebox holds creepy things like bones and dead bugs. There's even an entire cat skull.

"Lionel. We definitely found a witch," I say. I put the skull back with a shudder.

"Yes, most certainly." Lionel gestures at me to come over. He's broken into Marcus' private email. It's a hotbed of witch activity. An email thread from yesterday provides us with a couple of names.

Re: Meetup

i have practice @ 6 but can come after. tell bryant i got his plants so he better pay me lol

"Some things don't improve even with magic," I joke. The original email reads:

Meetup

All are called at 7:30. Bring your supplies. If you're out of anything, let Jacqueline know and she will acquire it for you before then.

- Head

"So he was part of a coven. Which one, though, if we're assuming this is a turf war?" I ask.

"He watched Kellan die and did nothing. I'd imagine they were members of rival covens."

"What could he have done in front of Natalie?"

"Would you let me die to keep the supernatural a secret?"

I shake my head. Never.

"My guess is that he was using Malani's interest as an excuse to make sure the spell worked. And, if that is the case, we need the guest list from the Royalty Masquerade Ball to see if any of these names are on it."

He spends the next hour poring through the email and getting names while I go "interrogate" the roommates. Neither of them, fortunately, is Bryant.

"So he just didn't come back last night?" I ask.

"Said he was going from practice to a date and we haven't seen him since. He's probably at her house, man. Why are you already acting like he's been gone for days?"

I'm interrupting their video game mission, you see.

"Because he disappeared off the face of the planet, you freaking gorilla," I growl. I'm so good at this. The guy pauses the game and stands up slowly to tower over me; he's twice as tall *and* twice as wide as I am.

"Whoa, dude, police," his pal whispers. He grabs the guy's arm and drags him back down onto the couch. I try to act like that's not a huge relief.

"Anyway, so you got any idea what the date's name was?" I ask like nothing happened. The big guy ignores me, going back to his game, but the roommate seems pretty eager to please.

"He hangs out with this cute Indian chick sometimes, and they go off to do group things a lot. I think her name is Melon or something." He smiles widely at me.

"I think you're thinking of Malani Abdul, who reported him missing," I fudge just a little bit.

"Yeah, that's it! These days, she'd probably know," he replies, nodding sagely.

"TV says you can't report people missing until they've been gone forty-eight hours," the other guy mutters mutinously.

"Technically, no, but there's been some weird stuff going on lately and we're trying to stay on top of things." I try to look tough and professional. "Plus, come on, man, she sounded really worried."

They don't seem to know much else about Marcus' personal life. Apparently the guys are all living together due to convenience, not brotherhood.

"Does Marcus ever bring anyone home? Friends or girlfriends, besides Malani?" I ask.

"One time he had a party, but we weren't invited. It smelled weird when we got home, but I figured it was, uh, some very legal stuff. Like from a hookah or something."

"Did he say what kind of party it was?"

"No, but he asked whether any of us were allergic to cats."

Bingo. "Why would he ask that?"

"Dunno, but there was cat hair all over the couch afterwards."

I resist asking what color. I'm doing good - don't need them getting suspicious.

"So Marcus doesn't primarily hang out with the football team?"

"He does, but we've all got our own friends too. Tell ya what, though, he spends way more time with his other friends lately."

"How much lately?" I ask sharply.

"Like, maybe a couple of weeks? Haven't seen him much outside of practice, and we live here."

I spot Lionel coming down the stairs and tell the guys I'll be in touch if I have any more questions. The friendly one seems okay with that, but the big guy gives me a look that could cut me if I got too close. Lionel waits until we're outside to ask why.

"I called him a gorilla."

My partner is too well-mannered to actually facepalm, but I can see that he's doing it in his head. I change the subject by telling Lionel everything I learned.

"So I think this turf war only goes back a couple of weeks," I finish. Lionel nods, looking thoughtful.

"That coincides with the largest wave of emails between Marcus and his coven. They were sporadic up until sixteen days ago and then suddenly there are email threads every day. Something happened between rival witches." He glances at me sideways. "And Malani is involved. Good catch, my friend."

"And people assume I'm the one who's distracted by big eyes," I say triumphantly.

Lionel chooses not to comment on that. "I have five names here that were in various email threads. We shall hope that they aren't aliases. Bryant, Jacqueline, Roman, Louis and Karen. Jameson's contacts are checking the ball's guest list for any of those names, but if Malani is in the coven, she may have been the only one present."

"If Malani is in the coven, though, why would she report Marcus' disappearance to Cecily?"

"They may be trying to draw Cecily out. To dispose of her before she chooses a side." Lionel's face is grim.

"So you think Marcus isn't dead."

"Not before I've seen his corpse with my own two eyes."

"We should check Natalie's house out, too. I doubt she's a witch in that coven since she's dead, but we should find out for sure." I quicken my pace towards the car.

"PATRICK, LOOK OUT!"

I dive to the side just as the sidewalk directly under me splits and yawns open with an ear-shattering crack. The whole area rumbles and shakes, and throws me off-balance when I land, but fortunately doesn't keep me from avoiding the hole. As quickly as it started, it stopped.

I get up and slowly move over to the gaping hole in the ground. It's probably a good ten feet around and I can't see the bottom. Broken pipes are pouring brackish water down dirt walls into the blackness, but I'm not hearing it hit the ground. I imagine I can see orange light at the end.

"Jesus."

"Patrick!" Lionel grabs my sleeve and yanks me around. He checks me for injury. "Are you unhurt?"

"Yeah, I'm fine."

My partner looks down at the hole.

"Patrick...I think the kid gloves are off."

***

"They tried to kill you with a sinkhole?" Cecily sounds incredulous over the phone.

"Yeah, I actually feel nervous anywhere now." I sip my coffee. Delicious, calming coffee.

"Cecily, could they do that again?" Lionel asks. He's stealing glances at me every so often.

"I'm not sure about the logistics of a spell like that. It's probably another that would take more than one witch casting. Where are you now?"

"The little cafe' across from the school. There is quite a crowd surrounding us," Lionel tells her.

"Good. It's a little odd that they'd try something so easy to avoid. It might have just been a warning that you're getting too close and they want you to step off." She sighs into the phone. "Well, in any case, I found out who Jack's owner is and you're not going to believe it."

"After discovering that the stupid jock is a full-fledged witch capable of killing people? Hit me." I rest my forehead on my palm.

"Natalie's parents: the Carters. Her mom works from home and her dad's some kind of businessman. They live about three blocks from me."

"What are the odds?" Lionel comments.

"Check both her house and her next-door neighbors. If she has small siblings, check their babysitters," Cecily suggests.

"You seem very calm about Malani and Marcus," I say.

"This isn't my first rodeo. Come over when you're done at Natalie's." With that, she hangs up. I lock my eyes onto Lionel and stare, waiting for him to stop smiling like an idiot.

"Wonder what other rodeos she's been in," I say. "Other stuff she isn't telling us, no doubt."

"I can hardly think much of the opinion of a bigot," Lionel sniffs.

"That makes you a bigot. You're prejudiced against bigots."

We glare at each other for a long moment.

"Lionel, you don't know anything about her except that she's dangerous and a liar," I say.

"My eyes are open. I am not a child, Patrick, that you have to protect. Besides, I merely think that she is attractive and intelligent. If she turns out to be our enemy, then I will act accordingly. You have always been able to count on me and this will not be any different."

Great, now Lionel is mad *and* hurt. This is why I don't let myself develop feelings for anyone. It always leads to strife.

"Let's just go." We leave the cafe', watching for any strange phenomena. I even keep an eye on the sky - for all I know, our witches have been watching cartoons and one of us might get a safe or a piano dropped on our heads. Makes me wonder how the city is going to explain that giant hole in the ground.

Natalie's parents live in a very nice neighborhood with lots of trees and little space between the houses. A small white dog starts yapping at us immediately when we set foot on the sidewalk leading up to the house.

"Lily!" A rotund woman with curly blonde hair comes bustling out of the door, shaking her head at the dog. Her makeup can't hide the blotchy redness around her eyes. My heart goes out to her, but I remind myself that it could be an act. After all, she owns the cat that almost got Lionel killed.

"Mrs. Carter. I am so, so sorry for your loss," Lionel says sympathetically as we approach the woman, who has picked up the dog and calmed it down. She nods and sniffles a bit.

"Thank you, Mr....?"

"Davidson. I teach English at the university. I never had the pleasure of teaching your daughter, but I thought I'd come offer my condolences nonetheless," Lionel lies smoothly. "This is my brother, Mike. He teaches some of the P.E. classes."

"Charmed. Please, do come in. Would you like some lemonade?" Mrs. Carter asks.

"Why don't you have a seat and Mike here can fetch it? You look dead on your feet." Lionel puts an arm around her and guides her inside. I use the opportunity to take a quick look around the yard and porch. Nothing weird except the fact that everything in the garden is dead. Natalie just died, so grief as an obstacle to gardening isn't a factor.

I go into the kitchen ass Lionel settles Mrs. Carter on her couch and starts talking to her about Natalie. The wallpaper is checked yellow and white, and there are herb gardens in the two windows. Both dead. Otherwise it's perfectly cheery in here.

There's a soft meow and I turn to see Jack curled up in a blanket-lined box under one of the shelves.

"Oh, no. You stay back there, sir." I point at him and step back. I make sure to give him the evil eye. He starts to meow again and yawns mid-sound. Clearly I am intimidating.

I decide to ignore him, but I keep an ear out for movement as I silently open a few cabinets. Lots of dried herbs, but I think that's pretty normal for a kitchen (I wouldn't know, as I could burn Jello.) No skeletons or statues.

If I don't get out there, Mrs. Carter is going to start wondering where I am and what I'm doing. With a frustrated grunt, I open the fridge and pull out a pitcher of lemonade. As I start rooting around for glasses, I notice that Jack is watching me with an intensity that he wasn't displaying before. His claws are even furling and unfurling. I'm pretty sure he's about to attack me.

"Good kitty," I try. "Cute kitty."

His eyes narrow. Awesome.

"Come on, Jack-kitty, we're friends." I smile, and then remembered that's considered a threat to an animal. He stands up and starts slinking toward me. His eyes are fixed on mine.

I grab the pitcher and three glasses and make a beeling for the kitchen door. I'll have to cross the familiar's path to do it, but maybe if I can get to the living room, I can avoid having my blood drawn. I make it through the doorway before Jack reaches me.

"Sorry it took so long, had to find the--YOW!" I yelp as Jack throws himself at me. Lionel stands up quickly, but Mrs. Carter just smiles a watery smile.

"Oh, he likes you," she gushes. I look down to see that Jack has leaped onto my leg and hooked his claws into my jeans, not into my flesh, and is staring up at me adoringly. He even starts purring.

"Is it safe to walk?" I ask, forcing a smile.

"He'll hold on. Come on over here and I'll get him off."
Mrs. Carter puts the little dog, Lily, down. She promptly starts
yapping again. Lionel slowly sits down again and mirrors my
fake smile. I shuffle over and set the lemonade down on the
coffee table; Mrs. Carter leans over and unhooks Jack, who
keeps purring like a motor.

I glance at Lionel. He shakes his head minutely. Mrs.
Carter isn't our witch.

She talks while playing with Jack's paws. "My husband
is out right now, but he'll be back tonight. He hated leaving
me alone today, but he said 'life must go on.' And he's right, of
course. We need to grieve, but we can't let this take over our
lives."

Her voice is mechanical, like she's reciting something
more than actually believing it. I glance around at the photos
on the walls of the living room. They're almost all the
traditional pay-a-photographer-with-generic-curtain-
backdrop, with the exception of a couple of vacation photos in
the mountains. I'd bet anything that all vacations are
instituted by Mr. Carter, as are all family photos. Judging by
the way Mrs. Carter dotes on her pets, I'm assuming they're
all she gets to have to herself.

"Personally, though," she looks around like she thinks
someone will hear her, "I think I might die. This isn't how it's
supposed to happen. It isn't. The child is supposed to bury her
parents, not the other way around."

She's crying again, her face buried in Jack's stomach.
Stupid cat just keeps purring. I look at Lionel again with a

pained grimace. I'm not good at this kind of stuff. Lionel takes my meaning and turns to the devastated woman.

"Mrs. Carter, I have no children of my own, so I cannot fathom what you are going through in this moment. All I can do is offer you my greatest, sincerest condolences. If you need anything, anything at all, please do not hesitate to call me." He slides a business card onto the coffee table.

"And, hey, if your husband keeps telling you dumb shit about getting over it, it's time to step up and ignore it," I add. "See a therapist, Mrs. Carter. Don't you bottle all of this up inside."

Mrs. Carter looks up and stares at me while Lionel mentally facepalms. I shrug and put up my hands.

"Look, I call 'em like I see 'em."

"In any case, Mrs. Carter, we are both available to talk or aid you. Extend this to Mr. Carter as well, of course." The last two words aren't quite said through Lionel's teeth, but it's a close thing.

After we say our goodbyes and head out the door, Lionel gives me a good hard whap upside the head.

"Ow!"

"You are not a feminist. You are a Slewfoot doing your job," Lionel snaps.

"I can do my job and still be a feminist!"

"That poor woman has lost her daughter and your attempts to make her--"

"Mr. Davidson!" comes Mrs. Carter's voice from behind us. I forget to turn around, but luckily Lionel doesn't. The round little woman comes puffing up behind us.

"I do have something that I want to say. To tell anyone. Please."

"Of course." Lionel steps closer as she gestures at him to do so. He leans in and she whispers something in his ear. I pretend to watch a bird in a tree, though she has to know Lionel is going to tell me whatever it is. Out of the corner of my eye, I see him frown in that way he does when something is "very interesting."

Once she finishes speaking, Mrs. Carter gives Lionel a knowing look and then hurries off. Lionel sidles back to me and tries to look casual.

"Let me guess," I say quietly before he opens his mouth. "She thinks Mr. Carter killed Natalie."

Lionel's eyebrows go up. "Do you read lips now?"

"No, but it struck me as odd that she wanted whatever she said to be so secret. I assumed the worst."

"Yes, she believes that her husband murdered her daughter with magic, in fact. She told me that she was too afraid that the police would lock her away if she mentioned it. The strange behavior of the cat, the constant absence of Mr.

Carter, and the always-locked basement have peaked her suspicions."

I eye him. "I'm not sure how that adds up to Mr. Carter killing Natalie even if we have info she doesn't."

"Apparently he had been complaining about their daughter for weeks prior to her murder. How Natalie was wasting her life on cheerleading, attending the wrong classes, how she didn't go to the correct university in the first place."

"Or how she stumbled on his coven killing people and he couldn't take the chance she might trace it back to him."

"Well, we have more information. Mrs. Carter is unlikely to consider something like that. In any case, over the past two days he has been acting very strangely. Quiet, obtuse, muttering to himself, disappearing into the basement and locking the door."

"So you're telling me that we should break into Mr. Carter's basement." I sigh. "And we were almost to the car."

"We will need to cover that base eventually, but since we have passed ourselves off as mild-mannered teachers rather than detectives, I doubt Mrs. Carter would be too happy to find us down there."

"Maybe, but on the other hand, I'm sure she'd rather have someone else investigate it. She's not going to do it. Besides, why else would she tell you about it?" I point out. Lionel stops to think for a minute. He's really great with books, but he's not so good with people sometimes.

"We could ask her," he says.

"Come on, we're gallant, right?" I pound him on the back with a grin.

"You are going to get me killed."

That's not as funny as it could have been, since last night I almost watched him die. But I force my grin to stay in place as we turn around and head back to the Carters'. I let Lionel explain to Mrs. Carter what we're going to do. For all his inability to figure people out, they still seem to like him more than they like me. Must be the glasses. Or the hair. Women love long hair. I'd grow mine out if it didn't burst into untamable curls when I do.

I'm still ruminating about hair when Lionel grabs my wrist and pulls me around the back of the house. I notice that all of the window shades are down - if we get caught, Mrs. Carter is going to deny having ever seen us before. Goody.

The basement is actually a large storm cellar, with one of those doors on the ground that leads to a staircase. It's padlocked in three different places.

"That's not suspicious at all," I mutter as Lionel pulls out his lockpicks. It's only the work of a minute or two to open all three locks. Padlocks aren't exactly complicated. When we open the door, motion lights come on and light our way down the wooden stairs.

Jackpot.

The room is fairly large, about half the size of the ground floor of the house, and unfinished. Insulation poofs out in fluffy pink clouds from between rafters in the ceiling and the floor is bare cement. A bench with a toolbox is pushed carelessly up against one wall. Maybe Mr. Carter had been working on the basement and got interrupted by witchcraft.

Evidence of that is everywhere. There's a pentagram etched into the floor, with a wad of wax that was once a candle at each point of the star and rusty stains in the middle. Shelves on each wall hold jars and bags of herbs; a glass case against the far wall displays about eight different knives. There are books and pieces of fur scattered about on tables and a floor-to-ceiling statue of Hecate in the corner with a plate of small burned bones in front of her feet. The whole place smells faintly like a mixture of blood, burned flesh, and herbs.

"I think we found the headquarters," I whisper to Lionel, who nods. Suddenly, above our heads, comes the unmistakable sound of a door opening and closing. We hear voices: Mrs. Carter's and a man's.

"I believe," Lionel says quietly, "that Mr. Carter is home."

Chapter Six

We sneak towards the stairs leading outside and hope that Mrs. Carter can distract her husband long enough for us to get out. More voices drift to our ears, one female sounding vaguely familiar.

"The coven?" I mouth at Lionel, who shrugs and nods. If they catch us down here, we're dead. I pick up my pace as much as I can.

Then we hear Mrs. Carter scream, and a heavy thud. Lionel and I look at each other. His face mirrors mine - pinched with indecision. If we go up there, we'll probably die. If we don't, and Mrs. Carter dies, we won't be able to live with ourselves. Then again, if she's already dead, there isn't anything we can do for her.

We can't take that chance. I see it on his face at the same second that I realize it. Unfortunately, just as we turn to head for the stairs into the house, we hear a key in the lock, and someone pushes open the door. As though we have the same brain, Lionel and I both dive behind the statue of Hecate. It's very crowded back here.

"Just leave her. I'll take care of it." An unfamiliar male voice, strong and imposing, comes wafting down along with the pounding of footsteps on the stairs we were approaching.

"What if she wakes up?" another male asks. I take that to mean that Mrs. Carter is unconscious.

"Where would she go?" the first asks. "Who would believe that kind, trusty Mr. Carter has kidnapped an innocent coed?"

"Those cops who keep pestering everyone about everything," growls a third male voice. Marcus. I never would have guessed that he knew the word "pester."

"They will both die as soon as we're all charged up again."

"Not as long as Hawthorne is protecting them," a female voice chimes in. They're in the room now. I carefully lean around and try to see faces. I glimpse Marcus and an older, balding man with solid features and dark eyes that I assume is Mr. Carter.

"Hawthorne is not the reason that the blonde one didn't die. That was reflexes. Slewfeet are well-trained." Mr. Carter gestures out of my line of sight. "Put her there."

There's a thump and a muffled cry. I feel Lionel tense up next to me, but I can't see who was put where. My partner turns his head as much as he can and mouths "Malani."

Well, shit.

"Situate her. Good." Mr. Carter crosses in front of the statue, which lets me see where he's going. To my horror, he's heading straight for the case full of knives.

"Isn't Ms. Hawthorne going to be pretty mad that we killed her favorite student?" Marcus asks. I hear muffled screeching and the shuffle of feet against cement. A couple of curses and a thump, and the screeching continues but the struggle is over.

"Hawthorne isn't going to be around much longer regardless, so I'm not too worried about her reaction." Mr. Carter selects a large, wide blade with a serrated edge toward the hilt.

"And what is this supposed to do for us again?" the female asks. She sounds irritated.

"It will recharge our batteries without us having to wait, Jacqueline. You felt the drain, didn't you? The last murder was no mean feat. Now come together."

The room goes mostly silent as the witches shuffle into place. I can still see Mr. Carter, standing at a point of the pentagram with both hands, including the one holding the knife, raised above his head in a supplicating gesture. He begins chanting in a low murmur. The other witches quickly join in.

The pentagram slowly goes from dark etches in cement to glowing lines of violet light. If Lionel and I don't do something soon, Malani is dead. She's still screeching, but the chanting is getting louder and swallowing her noises of fear. Cecily said the only time to interrupt a spell is during casting. I struggle as silently as I can to draw my pistol. Honestly, the only thing I can think of is shooting Mr. Carter. Maybe if I do that, the rest will be too shocked to do anything before I can get them too.

Lionel tries to get out of my way so I can get a clear shot, but there isn't a lot of room behind the statue. My entire world centers around the base of the statue when it just barely tips forward. There's a half an inch of air between the statue and the floor. As it falls back again, making just the slightest scrapey noise on the cement, I can only pray that none of them notice.

Mr. Carter's eyes shoot open. They're glowing violet too. He slowly turns his head to look in our direction.

I shove the statue over and shoot him in the forehead. Blam, right between the eyes! Damn, I'm good.

Since I hadn't been able to see the others, I have to aim before I can shoot at them. The statue hits the floor and shatters, which I guess knocks the rest of the coven out of their surprise because they all dive to the side. I get a bullet off at a wiry young man with glasses, but he manages to throw himself to the ground.

"Everybody freeze!" I snarl. The room goes still. I glance down and see that Malani is tied up and gagged in the middle of the pentagram. Tears mark her cheeks and soak into the fabric around her mouth. Marcus is there with her, holding her down while squatting with his feet planted on either side of a glowing line. His teeth are bared like an animal's.

"Don't look at me like that, you evil little freak," I snap at him. Lionel steps forward.

"Back," he says flatly to Marcus. The boy doesn't move.

"You're going to be so damn sorry," he says.

"I think not, but Patrick is, as you can see, willing to shoot. I would do as asked, Marcus."

His face breaks into the scariest grin I've ever seen. It's totally, completely manic. There's also something weird going on with his eyes, but they're dark enough that I can't pinpoint what it is. I swing my gun around to shoot him.

He has a knife in his hand and he embeds it in Malani's back. She arches and screams behind her gag, her eyes wide with shock. I fire, but Marcus is already gone, flinging himself at the dirt walls. As I fire at him and keep missing (why is he so damn fast?), the earth yawns open and swallows him like a giant mouth.

"Marcus you SHIT!" the wiry guy howls, banging his fists against the ground. The girl witch is huddled in the corner - her eyes are wide and terrified. The other two, a boy and a girl, are hiding under the stairs leading outside. They must assume the door is locked, or I bet they'd be gone.

Lionel is tending to Malani, but I can see by the grim look on his face that there's nothing he can do. Her eyes are half-closed and already blank; her chest stops rising and falling. Anger builds up around my heart and all I want to do is shoot every one of these witches.

Lionel closes Malani's eyes and stands. He's shaking.

"You have just participated in the murder of an innocent girl for supernatural purposes." His voice is quiet as his eyes travel over every remaining witch. "Patrick and I are well within our jurisdiction here and thus also well within our rights to kill you. If you wish to live, you will tell us everything we need to know."

"I want all of you on the ground, flat on your stomachs, with your hands behind your heads. Any movement other than that and I will shoot you. And somebody turn that off!" I gesture at the pentagram with my gun. The lines in the floor are still glowing, though more faintly than before.

"Please... it'll turn off on its own with no power running to it," the girl under the stairs whispers. She crawls forward on her hands and knees to lay down in front of me. She's a tiny thing, with curly reddish hair and big blue eyes. She certainly doesn't look capable of murder, but then, who does?

"Excuse me if I don't believe that it isn't going to just blow up or something," I say, rolling my eyes.

"I promise," she tries, pressing her face into the cement and putting her hands behind her head. I don't really have any choice but to believe her. It's not like I want them touching the thing.

"Fine. You too, shorty," I snap at the boy under the stairs and point at the spot next to the girl. He crawls out as fast as he can, stumbling and hitting the floor a couple of times in his haste. He's kind of chubby, but his hair and eyes are the same as the girl's. Twins.

When the wiry guy moves closer to me, I can see that he's stereotypically nerdy-looking with sharp features and the telltale signs of acne still dotting his face. The dark-haired girl in the corner lays down. Her entire body is visibly shaking.

None of them could possibly be over twenty.

Jesus. I glare at Mr. Carter's corpse. It seems pretty obvious to me that he tricked these kids into this. Probably just promised them magic and power. Twisted their minds. I'm glad that I killed him.

"My first question, I feel, is obvious: Marcus is not a witch, is he?" Lionel begins. The wiry kid shakes his head; Lionel turns to him. "State your name, please."

"Bryant Jacques. Marcus is a sorcerer. He joined our coven to help us with power."

That was why Marcus hadn't needed to stand at a point on the pentagram and why I'd noticed something weird about his eyes.

"Thank you, Mr. Jacques. Please explain to me what on earth you are all doing, murdering your classmates?" Lionel's voice is hard. The dark-haired girl speaks up.

"Jacqueline Frank. They started it by killing Angie."

Whoa. Hold up.

"Angie Collins was part of your coven?" I ask.

"Yes. We found out she was a target too late to save her. Marcus stepped in and gave us the power to kill two members of the opposing coven." Jacqueline's voice is dead and flat.

"Why did you not ask for the power to save Angie, rather than take an eye for an eye?" Lionel asks sharply.

"Marcus only knows how to attack and Head doesn't know how to use magic for defense."

"Mr. Carter isn't Head?" I ask, confused.

"No. He was second. Head has already fled town. We don't know his name."

I curse. "And you stayed and kept murdering people?"

"He said he'd kill us if we didn't finish it!" the round boy wails from his place on the floor. Glancing up at Lionel, he quickly blubbers, "Louis Kincaid!"

"Of course he did," I mutter.

"Karen Kincaid. Please, sirs, Jacqueline is lying," Louis' sister says. Jacqueline's head swings around even from its place on the floor. She glares daggers at Karen, but the other girl doesn't look at her.

"Oh?" Lionel squats down in front of Karen. I train my gun on Jacqueline, because she looks like she might actually throw herself on her coven-mate.

"I mean, yes, other witches killed Angie and we went after them, but--"

"Shut up, Karen! They're going to kill us anyway. I was trying to send them down the wrong path, you idiot!" Jacqueline snarls, spittle flying from between her teeth.

Karen stares up at me. Her eyes are wide and very blue. "Really?"

I consider. This girl has, with her compatriots, done some horrible, unacceptable things, even if they were under duress. But the fact remains that 1) she's a kid and 2) she's been brainwashed. Before I can answer her, though, Jacqueline speaks again.

"Oh, yes, Head told me all about you," she says. "You don't take prisoners. You just kill anyone who's doing something you don't believe in."

"Actually, we kill anything that's using supernatural abilities to murder humans," I correct her.

"But we only killed witches! This was a private battle. What right do you have to interrupt it?" Bryant interjects. I look helplessly at Lionel. We'd originally gotten on the case thinking that it *was* humans being killed, but the kids had a point: Angie, Kellan and Harold had all been witches in complete understanding of what was going on.

"All may have been well, but you have not killed only witches. You murdered one human child and then taken it upon yourselves to use the lifeblood of another innocent in an attempt to murder us," Lionel says, his voice devoid of emotion. His face might as well be made of stone. I have a harder time hiding my feelings about things like this.

Jacqueline opens her mouth again, but Karen cuts over her.

"They're right. We broke laws that would bring them down on us. If we'd just kept it in the coven, this wouldn't be happening." She has tears in her eyes now. It makes them look bigger.

"Correct." Lionel stands. "We also overheard a threat against the life of Cecily Hawthorne, who, while supernatural in nature, has n--"

"We didn't threaten her! She left us alone!" Bryant interrupts.

"Carter stated that she would 'not be around much longer.' Was that not a threat?" Lionel arches an eyebrow.

"Sorcerers never stay in one place very long. He meant she'll be moving soon. Why don't you do your homework?" Jacqueline snaps.

I start to ask why, but Lionel stops me with a shake of his head. Those are questions we can ask Cecily.

"Now, would anyone like to tell us what is actually going on in this town?" Lionel asks, glancing around the room.

"No." Jacqueline puts her face down, and with that, so do the other three.

"If you do not aid in the capture of your leader, then by supernatural law of which we Slewfoot are enforcers, you will be hereby found guilty and condemned." Lionel draws his own pistol and checks it; he looks professional, so the kids would never guess that he can't hit a wall from two feet away. I glance at him and meet his eyes. He nods.

I raise my gun and put a bullet in the cement right in front of Jacqueline's face. Shrapnel flies up and cuts her in about three different places. She jerks back and curls up, whimpering softly.

"We are prepared to offer you all amnesty if you answer our questions to the best of your ability. You will hereafter be watched for your entire lives. If you put a single foot out of line in the supernatural way, you will be executed on the spot with no leniency." There's still no kindness in Lionel's voice. Louis is sobbing noisily, but Karen nods. Jacqueline is still too afraid to look up and Bryant is staring at my gun with his mouth hanging open.

Karen is the one to begin. "What do you want to know?"

"One: what is the location of Head?" Lionel asks.

"We don't know. None of us knew where he was going. I'm sorry." Her eyes fill with tears again. She thinks we're going to shoot her because her boss didn't deem her worthy of such information. For an instant I feel guilty, but then I remember that the girl on the floor helped kill at least five people.

I cock my gun just in case. But Karen closes her eyes tightly and Louis curls up into a little ball, shaking. If they're shamming, it's pretty good acting. More than likely, they really don't know.

"Anyone?" I ask, looking around at the other two. They shake their heads.

"All right," Lionel says finally. "Then tell us the truth about the goings-on here."

"Culling," Karen whispers. "It's a culling."

Chapter Seven

We allow Karen to sit up while we question her. Louis, I'm finding, is a useless little lump, and the other two are quite willing to let Karen do the talking.

After several years of careful training and cultivation of the coven, Head had announced that a culling was in order. If a witch didn't have what it took to kill, maim, or otherwise fight, he'd said, they were no witch at all. Anyone who refused to learn "the blackest of arts" would leave.

In that vein, Head had, with the help of rogue sorcerer Marcus, bullied the coven into killing Angie, Kellan, and Harold once they had refused to be part of it and deserted. The others had been too afraid of Head and Marcus to refuse.

We ask them about the previous deaths, but as they'd all been wee things then, they don't know anything about them but assume they were part of the same practice. Head has been around for a long time, Karen tells us. He's good at recruiting those he sees potential in. None of the current coven was born in this town, so none of them knew about the previous deaths until it was too late to escape his clutches.

Mrs. Carter comes to during the interrogation. Fortunately, we hear her come running for the stairs and are able to intercept her before she sees the mess of bodies. Lionel explains to her what happened as carefully as he can, trying to keep from her the things that will get her in trouble. While he does that, I continue to question Karen.

Malani had come across the coven's activities before any culling happened. Knowing she'd be useful, Head had invited her in and allowed her to watch rituals, promising knowledge of the supernatural for her blog that would skyrocket her into fame as a paranormal investigator. The innocent girl had been completely taken in. Marcus had befriended her as well, but kept his sorcerer nature from her in order to keep a close eye on her. He'd waited and watched, pretending to be a guy pretending to be interested in Malani's hobbies, and then sprung when they needed her.

"This got out of hand. Even Head admitted that. He said we should keep fully unmagical human blood around in case we needed it, but I don't think he was expecting Malani to bring other people into it when he'd told her not to. He's so used to being too intimidating for disobedience, I guess." Karen stares resolutely at the floor. "So we had to kill that Natalie girl and Malani both, and with your being here and in the way, we needed to kill you too."

"He's had experience with Slewfeet before," I say, nodding.

"I guess," she replies.

"Why didn't he wipe out Cecily when she moved in? It seems to me that someone like Head would find her to be competition."

Karen snorts. "He says she's a mediocre spell-slinger who's too cowardly to stick her head out long enough for it to be chopped off."

Finally, someone who agrees with me.

"How would he know that?" I ask anyway, feeling that since Cecily is the reason my best friend is alive, I should defend her.

"Marcus said that she ran and hid when someone she loved was killed. He said all sorcerers think she's nothing." She shrugs. "I figured he must be right, since she never came after us."

I think of Sas and Lyla and how Cecily adores them. How she doesn't want to leave them without a mother. I don't agree with her, but I guess I can see where she's coming from. Someone like Head or Marcus would never in a million years understand something like that. Sighing, I move on to the next line of questioning.

"Do you have any idea where Marcus would go?" I ask her. She thinks for a moment, brow creasing.

"I'm assuming you know where he lives, so probably not there. Maybe Malani's house?"

"You're just guessing," I say flatly.

"Sorry. I'm afraid you'll shoot me if I can't answer you."

I'm losing her on the fear factor, actually. I can tell by her flippant tone.

"I'm not going to shoot you for not knowing something. Only for lying," I tell her. I start to ask her something else, but Lionel comes back down the stairs.

"They're here," he says. There are four men in a line behind him. They're all in suits, and are dark-haired and nondescript. Behind them come another four, but while they're dressed in the same fashion, you'd never think they were human. They're slightly... buzzy. It's kind of like looking at a static-y TV. Their shapes waver and tic like mad. When they reach the basement and there's room for them to spread out, each buzzy man comes to stand beside a regular guy.

We call them Lookers. A partnership where one is dead and one is alive. If we need to keep an eye on someone like these kids, Lookers are the ones to do it. Between each set of partners, they can blend seamlessly into any background. The kids will never know they're there - except that they know they're being watched.

And if they do step out of line, the Lookers will take care of it just as efficiently as any Slewfoot pair.

I gesture at the kids to stand and follow the Lookers. I doubt I'll ever see them again, but a "goodbye" seems pretty inappropriate under the circumstances. They all walk away and up the stairs without looking at me.

"Jameson is sending a crew to clean this up," Lionel informs me after they're gone. "Meanwhile, he also has his sources keeping an eye out for Marcus."

"I got a description of Head from Karen. Have Jameson put out eyes for him too."

We go out the other way. Lionel has put Mrs. Carter to bed and asked her to avoid reporting anything as long as possible.

"I'm not positive that she will adhere to that, but we can hope."

"Did you tell her what to report when she does?"

"Simply that her husband is missing. I have informed her that they will never find him and he will be presumed dead."

"Did you tell her that he is dead?"

"She didn't ask."

I wince. "Ouch."

"Are you all right?" Lionel isn't looking at me, but his overly casual tone tells me that he'd like to.

"After shooting a guy and scaring the shit out of a bunch of kids? Eh, not really, but they *were* murderers." In reality, I am feeling pretty shaky. We're usually after things that are either dead or don't look human, and if they do look like a member of our species, they aren't really. I'd just executed someone who'd dabbled in the supernatural but was, in essence, human.

Though I do firmly believe that he deserved what he got.

"The law was broken, innocents died, and if we had not been here, more would have followed," Lionel says firmly. He knows exactly what I'm thinking.

"I kn--oh, come on."

Our car has been dropped about halfway down a sinkhole.

"But we were standing right there with them! How did they pull this off?" I whine.

"Perhaps it is only the work of Marcus. It must have been he alone that made the attempt on your life at the school. Killing Malani may have recharged him, like a battery." Lionel sighs. "At least it was a rental."

"What about Malani's parents?" It suddenly occurred to me that I'm not sure how stuff like this is resolved.

Lionel's mouth settles into a thin line. "She will be found in an alley and her wallet nor her mugger will ever be located."

I shiver. It's all so cold.

"We will find the ones responsible for this," Lionel promises. I'm not sure if he's swearing it to me or to Malani's memory. I'd like to think it's a bit of both.

We wind up walking to Cecily's in silence. I haven't told Lionel what Karen said about our sorcerer ally and I don't think I will until I hear something about it from her. Personally, I'm so mad at Cecily that the idea of seeing her face is making me kind of sick. If she'd gotten involved, Malani might still be alive.

I know, I know, that's sort of a huge leap to make. I guess I'm just all-over angry. I'm angry at Head for brainwashing kids. I'm angry at Marcus for killing an innocent girl and for fooling us so completely. I'm angry at Cecily for staying out of it all. I'm angry at Lionel for seeming so emotionless. I'm angry at myself for not just shooting Marcus in the head when I first stepped out from behind that statue. Angry at myself for not being able to save Malani and Natalie. Angry at myself, hell, for being so angry.

So damn angry.

"Perhaps you should wait out here," Lionel says as we approach Cecily's doorstep. "You look a mite... infuriated."

I open my mouth to argue, but I'm interrupted by Cecily. She's standing in her doorway, ashen-faced with red rimming her eyes.

"Malani," she says softly.

"How could you already know?" Lionel asks, as confused as I am. Wordlessly, she holds up a little gold heart on a chain.

"It was left on my doorstep."

"Marcus," I snarl under my breath. Lionel nods.

"It must have been."

"Marcus? Marcus McKinney?" Cecily's eyes narrow.

"He murdered Malani in cold blood," Lionel confirms. "He is not a witch but a sorcerer, and a malicious one at that."

"He must be very old, to fool me like that." Cecily heads back into her house, leaving me to wonder what she means by that. Marcus can't be any older than she is.

Lionel follows her. I follow because I don't have anywhere else to go right now. I assume she has beer and will share.

Sas is dancing around in the hallway and whining worriedly. His massive rump nearly knocks me over in his determination to stay with his mom. I rudely push him aside to get into the kitchen to raid Cecily's fridge.

"Patrick," Lionel hisses at me.

"It's fine." Cecily has gone into the living room. Once I get my beer, I join my two colleagues. Lionel is about halfway through the story. I rub Sas' ears while he finishes. It's something to do with my hands. Out of the corner of my eye, I see that Cecily's fingers are running the gold chain over her hands. Her eyes are on Lionel, though - I don't even think she realizes that she's doing it.

"Your theory is correct," she says after Lionel finishes. "Marcus' murder of Malani recharged his batteries. He absorbed her life force."

"Is that something sorcerers do?" I ask, unable to hide the contempt in my voice.

"We can," is the short reply.

"I'm sure the power-hungry and evil are the sole users of this skill," Lionel interjects, shooting me a glare. I ignore him and focus instead on Cecily's noncommittal noise in answer.

"You've done it before," I accuse.

She finally meets my eyes. "When 300 years you reach, be so quick to judge, you will not."

I'm not sure whether I'm more shocked by the revelation of Cecily's age or by the reference. There's a long silence. Lionel recovers first.

"Sorcerers are immortal?"

"We stop aging at what our bodies consider our peak."

"So not only is Marcus not an idiot kid, but he's an evil bastard with magic powers and maybe centuries of experience," I mutter, throwing back my beer at the thought.

"There has to be another coven base. Head isn't going to go far and Marcus won't either. This can't just be about culling the more good-hearted members of the coven. It's too... precise. Attention-grabbing. Head had to know that this sort of murder would draw Slewfeet," Cecily muses.

"Has it every time? Maybe he assumed we weren't paying attention, since apparently he kills a few members of his coven every few years," I suggest.

"Something doesn't jive with Karen's tale. Why does Head require a den of murderers? If he were building some sort of witch army, he would recruit more than a few juveniles," Lionel points out.

"Or he's just picking the best of the best, or what that is in his eyes. You'd have to search records of who's moved from this town after school and that would be hundreds. Any of them could be witches, trained by Head."

The magnitude of Cecily's statement settles over us all like a ton of bricks. The more I think about it, though, the odder it seems to me.

"You think Head is raising an army?" I ask, incredulous. "How did you even come to that conclusion?"

"Why else bother with a culling?"

"Maybe he's just that evil."

Lionel holds up a hand to stop us. "Perhaps, instead of asking why, we should simply be asking where. The man, regardless of his purpose, must be found and disposed of immediately."

"I'd imagine that if you find Marcus, you'll find Head. You said the earth swallowed him? Then he's probably underground. Check abandoned buildings with basements." She leans down to pet Sas.

"Wait. After all this, after Malani is dead and the guy who killed her is the same thing as you, you're *still* not going to come help out?" I snarl, standing up to tower over her. She meets my eyes. Her own change into their catlike state.

"Are you saying that just because Marcus is a sorcerer, he's my responsibility? Is that because Head is human, so he's yours?" she asks.

"This is not a matter of prejudice. It's a matter of freaking decency and avenging the death of an innocent girl. You can help us, and you should. No matter how weak you must be or that your dogs might lose their mother." I throw my arms out, bringing Lionel into my words. "We don't know how to deal with magic. We have nothing to protect us except his brain and my ability to hit things. But we're going."

She looks at me levelly for a long moment. I'm still unnerved by her eyes - not just the weird cat-slit, either. I hadn't really noticed before that they're old eyes. Full of knowledge of things I'll never see. Before I knew that she was centuries old, I guess I chalked it up to being a teacher.

"You're brave men. Born to fight for your whole lives. I've lived your whole lives and more, and I've fought enough." Cecily goes back to Sas with that. Before I can argue further, Lionel grabs me by the lapel and drags me out of the house. He's livid.

"You do not have the right to tell her how to live," he says.

"She's a coward. All these years and she's afraid to die!"

"All of us are afraid to die. And you heard her, Patrick - she has fought enough battles."

I jerk my coat out of his hand. "There are always battles."

We glare at each other. I actually think, for a second, that he might hit me. Then he just deflates and looks at me reproachfully from behind his glasses.

"I understand that you are hurting, and angry, and tired of searching. But it is not Cecily's fault that Malani is dead. It is not her fault that Marcus is at large. It is not her fault that she was born something other than human."

I don't listen, but I do hear him. Instead of answering, I turn and head for the street. We'll have to catch a cab unless Lionel stole Cecily's keys.

Chapter Eight

We learn from the cabbie that downtown is full of old warehouses and office buildings, so we start there. It's quickly apparent that this will take all night if we don't narrow it down, so we have him take us to the library instead. Lionel is instantly in a better mood - he gets to do research. It won't take him all that long. When Lionel wants to know something, he finds what he needs faster than anyone I've ever met.

Me? I ask where the comic books are and disappear for an hour. The adventures of an angry duck alien on slightly-yellowing comic paper keeps me out of the world for a while, which is sorely needed at this point.

Still, an hour later, Lionel is still researching and the angry duck has finally gotten old. As this library lacks any superheroes of any kind in their comics section, I wander into the horror section. I know, it's weird that I like to read horror, given my job. It's interesting to me to see what other people think of when they want to be scared. I also take secret pleasure when an author is correct about a creature.

To my surprise, I find the cheerleading coach in there. And this time, she isn't wearing a tracksuit. Yowza.

She spots me at about the same moment that I spot her. "Oh, hello again, Detective."

Her smile is like a breath of fresh air. I plaster one on myself and walk over to her. She's got a copy of some obscure old horror novel in her hand. Something about a haunted cemetery.

"This is not the genre I would have guessed for you," I admit. She laughs.

"It's my well-kept little secret."

"So. Diana, isn't it?" My grin gets a little wider as she nods.

"And you're Louis. Did you get all of the information you needed about Natalie?"

Damn, she's talking about business.

"Well, I mean, yeah. We just covered the bases, but it turns out it was, well, a heart attack. Apparently they happen sometimes, just wham. Crazy."

She nods sympathetically. "I can't even imagine what that must be like. I also can't imagine what it must be like, doing your job. It must be so sad."

I force the image of half-open dead eyes out of my head.

"It can be, yeah." It comes out quieter and sadder than I meant it to, and Diana picks up on it.

"I'm so sorry. Let's talk about something else." She takes my wrist and leads me over to a little area of tables and chairs. At this time of night it's pretty empty.

"Sure, yeah. Tell me about you," I suggest. Is that a blush? I think it is. Man, I'm good.

"I don't do much besides read and coach. And yoga," she tells me. Her eyes are the color of coffee without cream, so dark they're almost black... like Marcus'. If her pupils change, I won't see it very well.

Great, now I'm getting paranoid.

"I get that. All I do is work," I say quickly, forcing myself back into the conversation.

"What are you doing at the library? Sorry, but you don't strike me as much of a reader," Diana admits with a little laugh.

"My partner wanted to do some research, so I'm killing time."

"Not the research-y type either, huh?"

I laugh. "No. He's the brains."

"It's nice to have a balance in a partnership, isn't it?" Her smile is a little wistful. Recent-ish breakup, I'd guess.

"In our line of work, it's essential. We have to work with each others' strengths and weaknesses or whatever we're doing could fall apart." I think for a second. "Or, you know, explode."

"Sounds dangerous."

"It can be that." I spot Lionel coming towards us out of the corner of my eye. Damn.

"Here." She's seen him too and hands me a piece of paper with numbers written on it. Score. I fold it up and put it in my pocket.

"I'll call you later, then. We can get dinner or coffee or something." I stand up and meet Lionel before he reaches us. He eyes me suspiciously, but when I smile winningly in response, he just shakes his head and starts walking toward the exit.

"In the middle of an investigation and you're flirting," he grumbles almost under his breath.

"She's pretty," I defend. "And she started it."

"She could be a spy. A witch."

"She could be. Or we can not be paranoid all the time."

"Says the hypocrite who exploded upon my infatuation with Cecily."

"To be fair, I didn't have a problem with it until we found out that she wasn't human and had-slash-has been lying to us from day one. Not even comparable, Lionel." How does he manage to make me feel petulant when I know I haven't done anything wrong?

He throws up his hands in defeat. "Fine. Now listen. There are only seven buildings downtown with unfinished basements, so we will begin with the nearest. Cecily seemed convinced that he would stay in an area he could easily escape in the same manner he escaped us."

"Should we call for backup?" I ask. "I know it's not normal protocol, but without any magical know-how of our own, we're going to need the help."

"I put out a call, but most agents are currently occupied. In fact, I was told by Command that the supernatural world seems to be in a bit of an uproar in general." Lionel's forehead creased a little.

"Did they say why?"

"They don't know, though of course research is being done both at home and in the field. We are quite on our own here, Patrick."

Well, if that's not a harbinger of doom I don't know what is. I hope we can take Marcus by surprise and just get it over with, because I doubt taking him alive is an option. Lionel apparently has the same thought.

"In, shoot, out," he confirms. "As much I would like to discover how much Marcus knows about the current state of the supernatural world, we have few resources and little time."

"Why do you think Marcus would know?"

"My impression is that any and all supernatural creatures are feeling the effects of the problem."

"So we can ask Cecily about it when this is over?" I keep my voice friendly, so he doesn't think I'm being mean or rude or whatever.

"Indeed. If it had not been for her grief-stricken state at the moment, I am sure she would have volunteered such information."

Is he trying to convince himself or me? Probably both. Personally, judging by her behavior, I think Cecily's loyalty is to herself and her dogs first, the supernatural world second, and Slewfeet last. For Lionel's sake, I can only hope that she might consider bumping us up a notch.

The first two buildings are busts. I'm finding this whole thing to be a huge cliche: skulking around big, dark, abandoned buildings and breaking into locked basements to find nothing but spiders and dust. I half-expect someone or something to jump out and attack us. In the second building, we do run into one ghost who halfheartedly rattles some chains at us before turning around and gliding through a wall with a distinct air of boredom. He can't get many visitors, so you'd think he'd be more excited.

"Chains? He's not even trying," I complain to Lionel. He just shrugs and hustles back to the cab to go to the next building. We're both twitchy with nerves, but I cover mine up with humor. Lionel just gets quiet at times like this.

I can't remember the last time we've been so unsure about coming out alive. The more basements we creep through, the more I realize that this is unknown territory. My hands are shaking and Lionel isn't talking. I start wondering what I've missed out on in life. A wife, kids, 2.5 dogs and a nice house in--wait, no, that all sounds like stuff Lionel would miss. Unless my subconscious is trying to tell me something. Either way, I resolve to call Diana tomorrow.

'If you see tomorrow,' my traitorous brain whispers. Of course, I have that thought as we tiptoe down metal steps to a basement where we can hear voices. I freeze, which makes Lionel stop as well. A cold sweat forms at my temples. You know, until it was staring me in the face, I was never afraid of death. Go figure.

We press ourselves silently against the concrete wall. My gun is up. Lionel is behind me, clutching a knife. It's the only weapon he's any good with, and even then, he's better with defense. I'm pretty much on my own if this comes to a fight.

The dirt floor beneath our feet may give Marcus an escape route, but it muffles our steps, too. There's no pause in the conversation in the next room. One of the voices is definitely Marcus, and goddammit, the other is a scared girl.

"P-please..."

Marcus giggles. Actually giggles. "Nope!"

"But I-I didn't do anything to you!"

"Doesn't matter!"

When he giggles again, it sounds like a bleat. I shudder. Lionel glances back at me. His eyes are worried.

I take a deep, slow breath to calm my nerves. I'm going to lean around and check for the sorcerer's position. If he's got his back to me I'll go ahead and shoot him. If not, I'll come back around and do it a second later. I think the element of surprise is all that will get Lionel and me out alive.

Marcus' bleating laughter continues, and suddenly the girl screams. So much for deep breaths and preparation. I throw myself through the doorway without thinking and bring my gun up to bear. I'm ready to fire, but there's no one there.

The room is empty. It's a cube of concrete walls and dirt floors with three empty doorframes leading into similar rooms. The only odd feature is a mound of dirt about a foot high piled up in one corner, but when I nudge it with my foot, nothing happens. The giggling and screaming continues, but I don't know which direction it's coming from. Lionel follows me when he doesn't hear a gunshot.

"Shit," I hiss under my breath.

"You go left. I'll go right," Lionel says.

"Splitting up is a bad idea. If there are hallways and you get in trouble, I might not be able to find you in time."

Lionel glares at me. "There is a young woman in trouble."

"And if you found them, what would you be able to do about it?"

"I could distract Marcus until your arrival."

"Yeah, he'll kill you in a second. Great distraction."

It takes us a second to realize that the screaming has turned into sobbing, though the giggling remains unchanged.

"This basement can't be all that big," I say and take off for the left door. Lionel, after a second, follows me, to my relief. The room is empty. I dive to the right and head across to the other one. This one is also empty, but it has a doorway leading to a second room. We barge through to that one. At this point, unless Marcus' laughter is pretty darn loud, I'd imagine he's heard us. So much for surprise.

This room is also empty, but before I can barrel through to the next one, Lionel grabs my sleeve. I barely manage not to shoot off my gun in shock.

"Patrick." He points at the floor. For a second, I don't see anything. Then I notice that the ground looks disturbed.

"Are you kidding?" I mutter. Marcus' bleating gets louder and the sobbing cuts off. I hope we're not too late.

"If a room was built down there, then there must be access in our general vicinity," Lionel reasons.

"Right." I glance around the room, but don't see any sign of stairs or an elevator. We hurry into the next room, but it's empty too.

"Is it possible, perhaps, that there is another floor below us? Nothing of the kind was indicated by the blueprints," Lionel mutters, stroking his chin thoughtfully.

"No, wait. It's buried." I grab his arm and drag him into the first room, where I'd spotted the mound of dirt in the corner. Together, we kick at the dirt until a metal trapdoor is revealed to be under it. It opens with difficulty and a deafening screech, which means that it probably hasn't been used in years. Marcus must have used the floor, even carrying a captive.

The stairs below the door look dubious; they're covered in a layer of rust with holes corroded into the metal, and they rattle when I lower my weight onto them. I half-expect them to just go crashing down and take me with them.

As I slowly and carefully climb down (no sense in getting hurt if I can help it), the screaming starts up again. It's ragged and permeated by more sobbing. I grit my teeth, leap down the last four steps, and take off down a dark hallway made entirely of dirt. The uneven ground still muffles my footsteps, but I'm sure Marcus knows we're here. That's probably why he's torturing the poor girl. Sadistic bastard.

As my eyes adjust to the dimness, I see pieces of peeling tape hanging off of the wall. There had been plans to add doorways and rooms to this hallway, but for whatever reason, the builders had decided to build the room at the end of the hall first. There's a light coming from there. Nowhere to hide, either; the doorway is an arch with no walls to hide behind.

It occurs to me that Marcus could have sealed it off. He wants us to come. The thought starts the cold sweat up all over again, but I don't stop.

He waits until Lionel and I are in the room before I hear the "thoom" of earth covering our exit. The circular room we've entered is about the size of a large walk-in closet with a ceiling that almost touches Lionel's head. There are bright lights strung up around the ceiling, though I can't tell where they're wired. It's not like an abandoned building has electricity.

The girl is tied up on the floor behind Marcus - she has tears streaming down her cheeks, which are marked with cuts and smudges of dirt. I recognize her as one of the cheerleaders from the college. She's dressed in a navy sweater and the remains of a short white skirt that's been slashed into tatters around her legs.

I see why she was screaming the first time. Marcus is... changed. His top half is the same, letter jacket and human torso, and his legs have torn themselves out of their jeans - morphed into what look like goat's legs. Shaggy brown fur covers them and they're tipped with black hooves the size of my hand.

"Fancy meeting you here," he giggles, a tiny bleat following his words. I can see now that his eyes are goat's eyes with the weird oval horizontal slit. They'd changed when he'd escaped at the base - that's what I'd seen, but I hadn't processed it as his true identity.

I get over my surprise at his transformation, lower my gun to aim right between his freaky eyes, and fire all in one smooth movement. No talking. This guy is playing for keeps.

A wall of earth shoots up and takes my bullet up into the ceiling in the blink of an eye. My shock freezes me, which gives Marcus a chance to grab the girl and pull her up in front of him. His big knife is in his hand, still stained from Malani's blood. It tickles his new prisoner's thigh.

"What is it you wish to accomplish here?" Lionel asks.

"I just like playing," Marcus answers in a sing-song voice. Creepy. "I've been around so long, I don't have anything else to do!"

Now would probably be a good time to fire again, but I'm about 98% sure that Marcus would just use the girl to block it. After all, he doesn't really need her as a human shield if he can use his magic. He wants me to try it. Part of the game is that I kill the girl to get to him.

I'm not playing.

Lionel and I should both be dead right now. We know it and Marcus knows it. We've got to find a way to use the fact that we're not.

"Why did you join a coven?" I ask. "You don't need them."

Just enough flattery to keep my pride.

"Why not? They could be used. I like using. I like death. I like chaos." Marcus lets out another bleating giggle. The girl has her eyes shut tightly, and I can see her shaking. We've got to at least rescue her. No matter what happens to us.

And I'm determined for Lionel to get out. He's a better Slewfoot than I am, anyway. Lionel's got more to live for.

That said, I'd *really* like to stay alive too.

"Come now, that isn't all you've got, is it?" Marcus taunts, the blade of his knife running up and down the girl's bare thigh. She whimpers softly as the sharp edge makes a shallow cut.

Lionel spread his hands placatingly. "What else would we have?"

I grit my teeth as more of my pride seeps away. I hate this guy.

"Sad. Sad. Because you see, if you don't entertain me, I'll get bored." The knife sinks in about an inch, and the girl lets out a little cry. Her leg jerks, which causes the knife to go even deeper. I wince in sympathy as she starts crying again.

"Perhaps you could let the poor girl go, and we could discuss this between three supernatural agents," Lionel suggests, keeping his tone calm and his face open. He's so good at this. I wish Marcus wasn't completely off his rocker so it might work.

"If I let her go, it'll be into the aether," Marcus practically purrs, pulling the girl a little closer. "No, no, in fact, I want you to meet your playmates."

Holes open in the ceiling, and four people drop through to land in crouches around us. Jacqueline and Bryant are among them; they both look unbearably smug. My heart sinks. I could shoot, but no doubt Marcus would defend. Best not to waste the bullets in case an opportunity does reveal itself. Nonetheless, I aim at Jacqueline, just to let her know that I've got her number.

"This is part of the game for you, yes? Pit two sides against one another and bet on who wins?" Lionel asks.

"Fun, ain't it?" Marcus giggles.

"Perhaps not the word I would choose."

A couple of the witches laugh nastily. Each one is holding a bone or a feather, which I bet are foci for whatever spells they've prepared. Jacqueline's sleek black feather is pulsing with light the color of an old bruise, and Bryant's bone is surrounded by light blue sparks that flash and fall to the ground. They burn the dirt wherever they land.

"I'll put my money on my coven, but you're Slewfeet. Surely you can pull something amusing out of your asses," Marcus says with a smirk. The girl slumps against him; we were her only hope.

The witches raise their foci.

That's when the dirt covering the exit explodes inward, showering us all with filth. I might never get it out of my white shirt, but I have never been so happy to see something blow up.

Silence settles along with the dirt. To my shock, it's Cecily standing in the now-empty doorway. Her cat eyes are blazing with fury and her hair must have blown back because it's just settling back to her shoulders - she looks like an avenging angel, even in her pajama bottoms. As my shock melts into something more manageable, I wonder how she blew up the dirt.

"Cecily Hawthorne. I admit, I wasn't expecting you." Marcus' voice is a little tense for the first time since I heard his real tones. The girl's eyes are wide as she stares at her teacher.

"I don't know how you've heard of me, but you shouldn't have riled me up." Cecily steps into the room. I feel... something in the air. It's like it's shivering in anticipation. The little hairs on the back of my neck stand up.

"Everyone's heard of you," Marcus says scornfully. "The one who always runs."

The witches look at each other in confusion. I think they're not sure how to deal with this unexpected new enemyThey still outnumber us, but Marcus sounds unsure despite his clear disdain. It's making them pause.

So I shoot Jacqueline.

It takes her right in the middle of her forehead. She's dead before she hits the floor, but it takes that long for the others to snap out of their shock.

Marcus snarls an order and three of the foci swing around to point directly at me. I fire at Bryant, but Marcus is ready with his dirt shields this time.

Except it doesn't help, because suddenly Bryant has been flattened against the opposite wall. I turn to see that Cecily has her hand out and her palm pointed at the witch struggling against the dirt. A twitch, and he lets out a little cry and goes still. His eyes are wide with fear now.

"Impressive. But can you deal with all of th--" Marcus begins, but then Cecily's free hand flashes a series of gestures - up, left, down.

One witch goes flying through one of the holes they entered through, his head cracking against the still-solid floor on his way up. Another slams into the left wall face-first and falls to the floor, unconscious. The last hits the ground with a yelp. Through it all, Cecily is holding Bryant against the wall.

"Let Stacey go or I will kill these two," she says. Marcus arches an eyebrow.

"But you're a good guy," he mocks. Cecily's eyes narrow slightly, and both hands twitch forward just a bit. Bryant lets out a strangled cry. The other one whimpers.

"Do you think, with my past, that I wouldn't be completely ecstatic to rid the world of two more witches?" Cecily says. There's so much rage in her voice that it makes me shiver. Lionel is staring at her with a new look in his eyes. It looks a little bit like fear, or at least trepidation.

"I think you've mellowed with age or there would be a lot more dead witches." Marcus smirks.

That's probably what sets Cecily off. I'm not going to describe what happens to the witch on the floor when Cecily's hand drops in a press-down movement. It's messy and loud, though quick enough that the witch's scream is cut off into a gurgle almost instantly. Marcus' captive screams and then faints. I taste bile and hear Lionel dry-heave behind me.

Bryant goes utterly white. "B-boss..."

"Shut up." Marcus drops the girl. His eyes are now focused squarely on Cecily. There's no trace of amusement left. To my surprise, when he drops the girl, Cecily drops Bryant. The boy crumples to the floor, gasping and coughing.

I guess I'd already forgotten, after that display, that Cecily *is* one of the good guys. I've got to rethink the company I keep.

"Patrick, Lionel. Get out," Cecily says.

"If you leave, I will kill the girl," Marcus snaps.

Decisions, decisions.

"Apologies, but as Slewfoot agents, we are charged with remaining to see the outcome even if we are not involved in the firefight," Lionel informs Cecily. He sounds a little breathless.

"Suit yourself." Cecily's eyes never leave Marcus'. I can practically see the wheels turning in his mind. Probably trying to decide whether to fight or flee.

I barely see it when he attacks. A huge chunk of wall breaks itself free and flies at Cecily at breakneck speed.

But her hand comes up too quickly. The earth slams against an invisible barrier and falls in pieces to the floor. Marcus tries again from the other side; same result. His lips are peeled back from his teeth in a grimace as he throws more and more at her.

It's like watching Cecily conduct an orchestra. Her hands move in time with Marcus' attacks and deftly block each one. He even calls up the ground below her, but pressing her hands down just causes the dirt to shift angrily before settling. I'm so busy watching that I don't notice when the ceiling above my head crumbles and starts to fall.

"Patrick!" Lionel yells. But Cecily already has me covered - invisible force throws me to the side just hard enough to get me out of the way as a piece of the ceiling collapses where I was standing. I land pretty hard on my bottom, but I can see cement in the debris on the floor. Cecily saved my life.

And her own, as well. When Marcus attacked me, he'd attacked her too. But she'd blocked it *while* helping me. Marcus, on the other hand, is panting and sweating like he just finished a marathon. Cecily looks at him with pity.

"You're way out of your league here, kid," she says, as though echoing my thoughts. "You're slow, you're predictable, and you can't even control your change."

"Who says I want to?" Marcus spits.

"Give up, Marcus. Let them take you in. I can and will destroy you."

I hear something I can't identify in Cecily's voice. She sounds... tired. But not from slinging magic around - that doesn't even have her breaking a sweat, unlike her opponent. Then it hits me.

Old. Cecily sounds old, ragged. Rode hard and put up wet, as they say. Suddenly I feel guilty for basically forcing her hand.

Marcus roars. Genuinely roars. The room shakes like there's an earthquake, and I definitely do not scream like a little girl when huge cracks start traveling up the walls and ceiling. Lionel throws himself at me and grabs my arm as he tries to physically haul me to my feet. But the shaking throws us both to the ground.

Bryant screams. I look over and then away before I see the piece of ceiling land on him - there's no way I'd be able to reach him, and I don't want to watch. The limp form of Stacey is thrown down next to me and the last thing I see before curling up over her and closing my eyes is a pair of pajama-clad legs.

Chapter Nine

I don't open my eyes until the world stops shaking. Honestly, I can't figure out why I haven't met the same fate as Bryant.

I understand, though, when I look up.

Cecily is standing above the three of us with her hands spread out over her head. I can't see a shield, but there's a perfect arc of dirt and cement pieces about a foot above her hands. She still isn't sweating, but she's breathing hard. I can see her legs shaking a bit.

"Hang on, guys, I've got this," she says, taking a deep breath. Lionel, still huddling over Stacey, bites his lip.

"Is there anything we can do to aid you?" he asks meekly. Cecily actually chuckles a little despite the situation.

"I wish. Just hold on to Stacey and your pants.""

Lionel grabs my lapel and drags me down over Stacey, closing his eyes again. I watch Cecily out of the corner of my eye.

She takes another deep breath and her fingers twitch minutely. The dirt and cement shakes as the shield moves outward. I have no idea how many pounds of rock are on top of us, but slowly, inexorably, Cecily's powers push it further away. After a minute, I can see light through the debris.

Cecily grunts and throws her arms upward. I gape as the invisible sphere expands in a rush of force and tosses the remaining debris away like it's made of paper. As it goes, I can see that Marcus' tantrum dropped at least the first two floors of the building on top of us. There's a cracked ceiling well above us that doesn't look long for this world.

The wreckage clears away enough for her to drop her shield. She doesn't exactly drop to the ground, but I can tell that she wants to.

"No time to rest." Cecily starts heading up the incline created by the moving dirt. I stand and pick Stacey up.

"Marcus?" Lionel asks as he gets to his feet. Cecily gestures at the wreckage around us.

"He decided to try taking us all out, even though he knew he couldn't control that much earth at a time."

"So he committed suicide rather than be taken in," I finish. Cecily nods.

"You might be surprised how many would take that option." Her voice is neutral, but the comment makes me wonder if she feels that way.

"Let us be off," Lionel says as the sirens get closer. Cecily's car is parked about a block away, and we manage to get there before the police and fire department arrive at the building.

Back at Cecily's, our sorcerer ally has me put Stacey in her guest bedroom, where she shuts the door and takes care of the wounded girl. Lionel and I tend our bruises under the watchful eye of Sasquatch, who sits quietly in front of the living room entrance. Lionel approaches him at one point and gets a tail wag for his affection, but it doesn't entreat the big dog to move. I marvel inwardly at his intelligence - he's guarding us.

Finally, Cecily comes down and flops onto the couch. Now that I'm looking at her straight on, I can see how tired she is. Holding up a few tons of cement and dirt will do that even to an incredibly powerful sorcerer, apparently.

That display definitely proved that Head has completely the wrong idea about Cecily. There's no doubt in my mind that she's not only a master of her element, but experienced and ruthless when she needs to be.

When Lionel opens his mouth to start asking her questions about everything that just happened, I jump in.

"Cecily, go to bed. We've taken care of the problem for now. We can deal with questions in the morning."

She blinks blearily at me. "What?"

"We'll just set up down here on the couch and floor again. You look half-dead."

"I'll be fine. I'm sure you guys want to head out first thing in the morning." She closes her eyes and lets one hand flop over the edge of the couch. Sas pads over and situates himself so that the hand is resting on his back. Lyla comes trotting in as well and yawns as she curls up next to Sas.

"No, Patrick is right. I shall make our report to our client and then repose as well. We have all had a trying few days." Lionel pulls out his phone. I can't help but chuckle as I realize that, despite her words, Cecily didn't even make it to the end of Lionel's sentence. She's out like a light.

My partner takes a blanket from the armchair and gently rests it over her. The two of us go outside to avoid waking her up. Lionel turns abruptly to me and crosses his arms. I blink at him.

"What?"

"She saved our lives," he says. I realize what he wants.

"Oh, come on, Lionel. What I did in there was an apology. You know that."

"She doesn't know you like I do."

"She just doesn't want a bad reputation. Lionel, you've got to realize that she doesn't care about us."

"How can you say that?"

"Lionel, she only came after us because I guilted her into it."

Lionel shakes his head. "Why are you so determined to believe that she is not our friend?"

"Because she's nonhuman! They don't think they way we do. They don't feel!" I snap before I can stop myself. Lionel's eyes widen a fraction.

"After everything she just did for us - you still believe that?" he asks with deep disappointment evident in his voice.

"Obviously."

"We are alive because of Cecily Hawthorne. For Pete's sake, why do her reasons matter? She still came for us." Lionel put his hands on my shoulders. "Please, Patrick, why aren't you hearing me?"

I close my eyes tightly. Lionel doesn't know much about my past because I don't talk about it. Flashes of teeth and blood and light explode in front of my eyelids.

I still remember my mother screaming as she shielded me with her body. I remember the smell of her still-damp-from-the-shower hair, the same color as mine. I can see my dad brandishing a baseball bat at the hulking creature in the doorway. I hear its snarl of challenge, and when my dad swings the bat, I remember the sound of it breaking in his hand.

I remember what it sounded like when he died.

I shake my head to clear it. "Look. I get what you're saying and you're probably right. It's just hard for me to accept that something supernatural could be so human. I'm not used to it. I've never seen anything like it before."

"It is human nature to fear that which we do not understand, Patrick, but you must look at her actions here tonight. She has proven herself an ally."

I meet his eyes, finally. He's so sincere and patient with me, like no one else ever has been. That's why he's my best friend - he balances me out.

For his sake, I'll give this a shot.

"I wonder if any pizza places are open. I bet you're starving. I know I am. Wonder if Sas and Lyla have been fed yet."

Lionel recognizes it for what it is. He lets go of me and manages not to smile.

"Let us check the phone book."

"Lionel, no one has a phone book anymore."

"Then the Internet."

"There ya go."

***

Cecily comes padding into the kitchen at about 9 in the morning, yawning widely. She's not even bothering to hide those creepy eyes of hers, but I keep my mouth shut. She flops into a chair and yawns again. Lionel brings her a cup of coffee and a slice of microwaved pizza.

"Breakfast of champions," she says before going at it. Sas and Lyla, who were treated with pizza last night, come trotting over to beg for scraps. Cecily eyes them and then squints at me. I grin and put my hands up innocently.

"Years of training down the drain," the sorcerer grumbles, going back to her slice. I pretend not to see her give each dog a slice of pepperoni. Lionel seats himself in the third chair and nibbles at a smaller sliver of pizza. We wait for Cecily to finish her breakfast; she looks more alert after that.

"Okay. What do you need to fill in the blanks?" she asks.

"First, we simply wanted to thank you," Lionel says. I sort of nod and look away. I'm not really good at the whole gratitude thing when I'm still trying to sort someone out in my head.

Cecily waves it off. "No problem."

"We understand that you would rather not have gotten involved," Lionel continues as though she hadn't spoken. "So therefore, we are grateful and now are in your debt."

I can tell that makes her uncomfortable. She's looking resolutely into her coffee cup and not at us. That just confirms my suspicion that she didn't do it for us.

"May I ask what changed your mind?"

I'm surprised Lionel asks. He seems determined to see her as a friend or at least an ally. He's got to know that her answer might change that. Maybe that's why he asked: to nip any feelings in the bud if he has to.

"A lot of things. First off, I wasn't lying when I said that I like you guys. Second, Marcus killed an innocent girl because it was fun for him. Third... I hate witches. I mean, I really hate them. Wherever I go, I don't ask for the coven not because I'm afraid." She meets my eyes. "It's because if I know who they are, I will go after them and kill them."

Well, that's a dark turn.

"Most of the time, witches are kids or misguided adults. They don't know that what they're doing is going to warp them into something like Head. They're so damn arrogant that they think they can control one of the most ancient, powerful forces in the world. In reality, it controls them. It's not their fault," she adds when she sees my face. "But once they're gone, they're gone, and there's no bringing them back. That's when they start using it to kill, and they'll kill until they're dead. You guys landed smack in the middle of some seriously dark powers."

"Why don't you ever try to find them? To steer them away?" I ask. I work hard not to put any condemnation in my voice.

"I do. I teach my classes."

I feel like smacking myself. Of course she does.

"Kids who wander into a coven are going to take a class on magic, don't you think?" She doesn't sound smug. Just factual. "Witches hate sorcerers and vice versa. I don't know if it's jealousy, or just a clash of magic types, or what, but it's like Israel versus Islam up in here. If I revealed myself to these witch kids, they wouldn't listen to me. But if I'm some human teacher who might know what she's talking about? Sure, they'll give it a go."

"So, basically, the two options are you teach them and they quit on their own, or you kill them later?" It pops out before I can stop it.

Her voice is deadpan. "I'm trying to quit, really, but it's so addictive."

"It's just an ingrained thing? You just... hate witches?" I ask, deciding that if the train was heading for a wreck I might as well make the most of it.

"I have reasons as well as the general animosity."

"Back to the important issues," Lionel interrupts before I shove my foot any harder into my mouth. "How did you discover our whereabouts?"

"I'm pretty sure we used the same methods to find out which buildings had dirt basements."

"Why was Marcus all... goat-y?" I interject.

"A lot of us can't control our physical forms while using magic and Marcus had been using his so much that he lost it entirely. If he'd lived, he probably could have shifted back in a few hours."

"How come you didn't go all completely catty then?"

"More practice."

"Do you have any idea of the whereabouts of Head?" Lionel asks to steer us back to what he deems "important."

"I wish."

I shudder a little. Cecily's not looking at me anymore, but her voice has gone cold. And from what I've seen, I do not want her pointing that anger at me.

"Shouldn't you be making a report or something?" Cecily asks Lionel.

"I have, to our client. All attempts to get through to Slewfeet headquarters are, however, busy signals only. I shall make another attempt shortly." Lionel sounds nonchalant, but I know he's worried. I am, too.

"We also have not heard from the Lookers assigned to Jacqueline and Bryant, who were involved in this most recent skirmish."

"I'll go with you to check on the other two witches. Promise I'll be good." Cecily puts her coffee mug down and hops off of the tall chair, padding off to get dressed, I guess.

"You tried the Lookers? Both sets?" I ask Lionel. He nods.

"They did not respond. While that is not uncommon among members of their sect, I still worry when I consider the strange happenings centered around our organization."

"How would you get rid of Lookers, though? I mean, one of them's a ghost and exorcism isn't exactly a short process. Plus, aren't they supposed to be basically immune to it?"

"Indeed. In order to keep them fully connected to this plane, their soul is tied to their partner's. Thus, exorcism would be unsuccessful and the human partner is, for all practical purposes, immortal. It is a mutually beneficial relationship."

"Sounds awful," I mutter before returning to the matter at hand. "So, what you're telling me is that there's no way Jacqueline and Bryant should have been able to get rid of their Lookers."

"They are quite beyond formidable, so indeed not."

"So something is extremely, totally not right."

"Indeed."

"Great."

Chapter 10

We start at Louis and Karen's house. It's a dump in a terrible part of town, with a sagging porch and plastic garbage bags covering several broken windows. Poor kids.

Their parents are skinny people with straggly hair and missing teeth. I can see bits of Karen in her mom's face. The woman had once been quite pretty. Honestly, I don't know where Louis was getting the sustenance to be pudgy. My guess is Head.

Mr. and Mrs. Tavor are helpful in that they get very angry with us very quickly.

"We already reported them missing! We were told that we would have to wait 48 hours for the police to begin looking. So screw you and the horse you rode in on!" The door slams in my face, which I'm grateful for because it cuts off the must-and-sex stench of the interior of the house.

"Well, at least we know that they're missing," I pseudo-chirp.

"Weird that they would be so rude to police when we came looking if they reported them missing," Cecily points out.

"Perhaps their ire was less directed at us for searching and more that our inquiries painted them as ineffective parents," Lionel says.

"How does 'Hi, I'm Detec--' paint them as anything?" I protest as we walk towards Cecily's car.

"I think he means that they feel like they've done all they can and the fact that we're doing more pisses them off." Cecily's voice is dry as a brittle leaf.

"Wish we'd known that they'd grown up in a place like this," I say as I look around at the dilapidated houses, broken toys and rangy strays strewn around the neighborhood. A bald guy with a saggy beer belly and a rusty Bowie knife glares at us from a porch that looks like it's going to come down any second. Dollars to donuts he's a drug dealer.

Cecily gets in the car and turns it on, not looking at me as she says, "Still not an excuse."

"They are old enough to know better," Lionel admits. I don't add anything, because they're right and that sucks. Still, I'm glad that we chose not to kill them. Lionel gets in the front seat, eying me like I'm going to fight him for it. Crushes make people act so alpha.

"Where do we go next?" I ask as I climb into the backseat. "We don't know where they would have gone."

"Perhaps another coven member's house?" Lionel suggests.

"With the Lookers on their tails? Though I guess they were probably scared and desperate."

"Think 'safe.' Where would be a safe place for a couple of scared kids whose every moves are being watched?" Cecily asks.

We all think in silence for a minute. The guy on the porch is still staring at us and I'm finding him distracting. He sees me looking at him and curls his lip to reveal a tooth that might have been white at one point, but I couldn't prove it. A mangy cat jumps up on his porch rail, settles in, and adds its glare to the drug dealer's.

I wonder, idly, how the Tavors ended up in a place like this. Didn't they have parents to teach them right and wrong? Someone to get them ice cream, hug them, take them to--

"The park," I finish my thought aloud. "Is there a park around here somewhere? A place they'd be familiar with that they might use as an escape?"

"Such a getaway would be the first place their parents would look, would it not?" Lionel asks.

"I seriously doubt those people have any idea what their kids get up to or where they'd go on a regular basis. But I bet Karen and Louis aren't usually gone this long, which is why their parents are scared enough to call the cops." Cecily has picked up my train of thought.

"In this neighborhood, they think something's happened to them. It wouldn't occur to them that Karen and Louis even have a getaway because that wouldn't be safe. But the kids do have one, and they can't get in trouble with the Lookers for going there," I finish. While we're talking, Cecily is driving along the road with her eyes peeled. There are enough broken toys lying around in yards that it seems likely there are lots of kids in the area. Surely there must be a playground.

We come up on a little grassy area with a faded sign that says "Knolte Park - No Dogs." The park is actually pretty well-kept for as crappy as this neighborhood. The grass has been mowed and there's even a little flowerbed along the edge, though the flowers in it are starting to die. There's even a jungle gym in one corner made completely of brightly-colored plastic, so less risk of tetanus, I guess.

We park in a little empty lot on the edge of the park and head in. A couple of trees rustle dying leaves at us as we walk, looking for any sign of Karen and Louis. Other than a lone shoe lying dejectedly by the side of the road, there's not much indication that people visit this place. Perfect for a couple of kids stuck in a rut of black magic and drugs.

"Guys." Cecily's voice is tight. I jog over and reach for my baton. The sorceress is standing over a patch of dirt that looks disturbed. Totally innocuous... unless you've just dealt with an earth-controlling sorcerer. The patch is about three feet in diameter.

"You don't suppose that the children are beneath, do you?" Lionel asks, sounding a little queasy. Cecily bites her lip and runs her foot over the dirt to shift it around.

"Only one way to find out," she says. I find a few sticks lying around, and we start digging. Apparently Cecily doesn't keep shovels in her car, go figure.

Despite the fact that we're looking specifically for buried kids, we all still jump like scared rabbits when, barely a foot in, the packed dirt breaks and cascades into a hole. We hear coughing and gagging.

I'm the first to recover. I kneel next to the hole and look down. A familiar pair of frightened blue eyes in a dirty, bruised face look up at me from a good six feet down.

"Karen!" I put my arms down for her to grab and she practically scrabbles up me in her haste to get out of the hole. I see a shock of red hair in the hole below her, but it's still. Karen buries her face in my shirt and sobs. She's gripping my lapels so hard that I'm afraid she's going to break her fingers.

"Louis, Louis," she cries. Lionel, who is now climbing out of the hole, looks at me and shakes his head grimly. He can't get the poor dead kid out. We're going to have to leave before the cops get here. Hopefully they'll believe that Karen got herself out.

"Marcus?" I ask her. She nods, clutching me even more tightly.

"He sh-showed up here and b-buried us w-without even s-saying anything," she babbles. "Louis b-broke his neck on the w-way down."

Jesus Christ. Karen's been trapped down there with her dead brother's body for almost 12 hours. Lookers don't make footprints, but there's no sign of them at all. Surely they would have tried to get the kids out, even if they assumed they were dead.

"Did you see what happened to your escorts?" I ask her, gently petting her hair to let her know that I care about her pain even if I'm asking about the Lookers instead of her health. She shakes her head.

"I never saw them after the first minute. I d-don't know where they are."

That doesn't bode well.

"I called an ambulance," Cecily informs me as she approaches us. "I hate to leave her, but we shouldn't be here when they arrive."

Karen looks at Cecily with big, owlish eyes. "Who are you?"

"Cecily." my ally replies. She's trying to hide her aversion to the little witch.

"Oh." Karen looks down sheepishly, leaning against me. I gently take her to the ground and get her to sit.

"Okay. We have to go before the police get here, but I want you to call me when you're ready." I press a business card into her hand. "We need to talk to you some more, but I want you to get medical treatment first, okay?"

She nods wordlessly as she stares down at the card. I guide it to her pocket and stand up. I can already hear sirens. No time to look for the Lookers right now, not until the park is clear, so the three of us leave the traumatized girl and hurry out of the neighborhood.

"I'd say that's a pretty good indication that they're innocent in the whole Marcus thing," I state as we drive towards Cecily's house.

"Good thing the sick bastard is dead," Cecily says.

"We are sure about that, right?" I ask just for clarification's sake.

"Oh, yes. Quite sure."

Her tone scares me, so I change the subject. "We should check out Jacqueline and Bryant for the same reason. Find out where their Lookers went."

"I shall have Jameson acquire their addresses." Lionel dials and turns away to the window for his conversation with our client.

Cecily and I ride along in silence while Lionel fills Jameson in. After a while I lean forward to put my head between them. It made me feel like a kid with his parents on a road trip.

"Did you find out in some weird way that you were a sorcerer?" I ask her quietly. "Or did you have nice parents who taught you everything you know?"

"My mother died in childbirth and my father threw me out of a window because of my eyes."

Awkward.

"Threw you out a window?" my mouth continues around the foot in it. "How did you survive?"

"I landed on some poor guy trying to sell bread on the road." To my surprise, she smiles. "He ran screaming, too, but a local sorcerer named Leonardo picked me up and took me home."

"I'm glad the story has a happy ending."

"As these things go, sure. Back in my day, kids born with anything weird on them were killed or abandoned."

I was about to ask how far back "back in her day" was, but Lionel was just hanging up. Back to important things.

"Jameson has retrieved the addresses. Jacqueline, it turns out, lived only two houses down from Malani."

We go there first. The house looks the same as Malani's - typical student housing. When we knock, no one answers. All of the lights are out and there's no car in the driveway. The three of us go around the back, where Lionel picks the lock on the back door.

It's the most Spartan interior I've ever seen. The kitchen has a refrigerator and a microwave. There is a couch and a lamp in the living room. One bedroom is completely empty and the other contains a neatly made bed with a laptop on it and a dresser. It's pretty clear that Jacqueline lived alone and didn't entertain.

Like Marcus, she had a closet full of creepy witch things in shoeboxes. I guess that's the container of choice for homicidal college students. As we sort through them, discovering the same sorts of herbs and bones as in Marcus', Cecily shakes her head.

"What a lonely person," she comments.

"Seemed like a choice, from what little I noticed about her personally," I say, picking up a rodent skull. "She and Bryant seemed to have a good evil thing going, anyway."

"I do hope you're joking." Lionel has hacked his way into Jacqueline's laptop. She has the same succession of emails as Marcus, but otherwise her inbox is full of coupons and school messages. No mention of the Lookers.

"This is slightly off-topic, but could we send Head's email address to Jameson and have him track the IP address?" I ask Lionel.

He manages, barely, not to look affronted. "Patrick, I have already tried that."

"Well, you didn't tell me," I say and go back to the shoebox.

"I apologize. Head is clearly masterful in the art of hiding, able to shield himself from both human and technologic eyes. Jameson found nothing."

"God, for a powerful witch, Head's a freaking coward." I sigh and stand up. "There's no sign that Jacqueline has even been here in the last few days."

"There are also no leads as to anywhere else she might travel," Lionel adds, closing the laptop and tucking it under his arm.

"Pillager," I say.

"Evidence," he lies easily. I don't know much about computers, but I'm guessing that must be a nice one if Lionel is steali--I mean, acquiring it as evidence.

We have a little more luck at Bryant's. He, at least, had stopped at home and ordered some Chinese food. We know it's from that night because he left his receipt lying on his dining room table.

"You'd think that being under what basically amounts to a life sentence, possibly a death one, would alter your appetite," Cecily observes as she counts three takeout cartons in the trash.

"If he knew Marcus would come to get him, he wasn't worried." I take the house in. It's a little bigger than Jacqueline's and has seen more use, if the scuff marks on the pastel green walls are any indication. He also has a decent amount of furniture, hilariously mismatched, and an expensive-looking TV with no less than three game consoles hooked up. There's a beat-up bookshelf holding a very impressive game collection next to it.

We head into the bedroom, which is painted light blue. The bed wasn't made and one of the dresser drawers is hanging open. I have my doubts that Jacqueline could have visited without throwing up.

Up against one wall is a spindly-legged desk bending under the weight of three flat-screen computer monitors. Lionel sits gingerly in the tattered desk chair.

"This may take some time, if young Bryant was as capable of a computer technician as he appears to have been based on his machines. Perhaps the two of you should search elsewhere."

Cecily and I wander the house, looking in cabinets and behind furniture. No signs of a struggle here either.

"It doesn't make sense," I say.

"Is it possible that your headquarters called the Lookers back and just didn't inform you?" Cecily asks. "I mean, there's a bigger picture."

"I doubt they've pulled Lookers, though. If it were something big enough for that, we would have been given more information about it. Don't you think they would have pulled us, too?"

"Well, unless they think Head is a big enough priority."

"If only I had the time and patience to call every Slewfoot I know and see if they're still sticking to their cases," I muse. Cecily rolls her eyes and starts shifting the couch by herself. When she bends over, I can see one of the reasons Lionel likes her. Assuming he's an ass man. Wow.

"I'm going to break your face," she says without turning around.

I start looking behind the TV nonchalantly, like I don't think she means it. Coincidentally, that's where we should have been looking.

The wall behind the screen is smeared liberally with slimy, thick, clear liquid. Ectoplasm. Only one kind of creature bleeds that.

"Lionel!" I yell. He comes running with his gun drawn for all the good it'd do him. He sees the ectoplasm before I have to tell him.

"Outside," he says and heads for the door. We follow, Cecily looking as grim as I feel.

We find Lionel squatting next to the wall of the house. He's examining a nasty pile of ectoplasm. The stuff is slowly sinking into the ground, but as thick as it is, it takes a while. Lucky for us. Not so lucky for the spirit.

"A ghost. Perhaps not the Looker, but certainly a soul of some sort," Lionel says for Cecily's benefit. I can see that she knows by the slightly arched eyebrow she sends him, but she doesnt say anything about it.

"How can we be sure?" she asks.

"Check for disturbed dirt," I say. "The ghost wouldn't have been far from his partner, so if the partner is dead, Marcus probably would have buried him."

We look all the way from the wall to the street, but the lawn is overgrown and clearly hasn't been touched by a lawn mower in weeks, much less knocked around by a sorcerer. It's all really confusing.

"So that's a different ghost?" I ask, gesturing at the ectoplasm.

"It would seem so. After all, Lookers can only be separated when they both die."

"So, what, Bryant picked off ghosts for fun?"

"Or the spirit discovered something Bryant preferred remain hidden." Lionel kneels down next to the ectoplasm again and uses a stick to sift through it. Ew.

Cecily leans over to look, and when she does, whatever's on her chain swings forward. It glimmers dully before she grabs it and shoves it back down her shirt. But I know Lionel's face, and he looks kind of shocked and intrigued. I make a mental note to ask him about it later. Curiosity probably killed the Slewfoot, but I can't help it.

"I think we should check the house again," Cecily says. "Maybe there's a basement or an attic."

We all troop back in and start looking. Sure enough, in the hallway, there's an almost-hidden door leading into an old attic. Once we get the ladder pulled down, I head up first, climbing one-handed with my other hand on my baton.

I didn't need to bother. The sight in front of me makes me freeze, right there crouched on the edge of the attic floor. The human Looker is unconscious and his ghost partner is floating above him. He's held somehow with his toes pointed at his partner's head and his face pointed at the ceiling. Even though he's insubstantial, I can see veins bulging in his neck at the strain.

"Holy Hannah," Lionel curses from behind me, or, you know, as close to cursing as he ever gets.

"Head," Cecily says, poking her head up next to Lionel's shoulder when she realizes he's not going to climb up any further.

"How do you know?" I ask her. I climb the rest of the way into the attic and step carefully towards the Lookers.

"Stop! Don't touch them." She practically shoves Lionel out of the way in her haste to grab the back of my coat. Lionel scrambles up after us with wide eyes.

"What would transpire?" he asks. I pull away from her, but I'm a lot more careful after her warning.

"I'm not sure, but since it would have to be Head who cast the spell, you can bet it would be nasty. Marcus only had the power to move earth and Bryant wouldn't have been nearly powerful enough to do this," she responds.

"Fair enough. How do we free them?" I circle them, and I think I see the ghost's eyes following me as much as they can.

"You'd need a witch for that. A strong one."

"Know any?" I ask off-hand, forgetting Cecily's hatred for a silly second.

"No." Her voice is clipped, and I feel chagrined. The look on Lionel's face doesn't help.

"What about a sorcerer?" I try. Cecily looks thoughtful.

"Well, I know a diviner. She can see how the ritual was done, and then we might be able to undo it without an actual witch's help."

"Okay." I turn to the ghost. Now I'm sure he can see me. I manage to remember his name. "We'll be back, okay, Hancock?"

When nothing happens, it occurs to me that maybe a) he can't move his eyelids or b) he can't hear me. I sigh.

"I shall remain here and discover whether there is other evidence I can glean," Lionel says. "While there is little I can do for Mr. Hancock, it seems imprudent to abandon him even for a short time now that we have ascertained his whereabouts."

I'm not surprised that Lionel's cool with me being alone with Cecily. He knows I'm repulsed by her otherness, and even if I weren't, he trusts me not to move on the woman he's interested in. As a kid, I'd always had friends, but none I'd refer to as my "best." Lionel filled that hole like he'd been made for it, and he felt the same way about me.

I realize, as Cecily and I climb down the ladder, that I'm thinking about those things because I'm worried. What if Head comes back while Cecily and I are gone? I'm pretty sure the sorcerer is the only one who'd have a chance against him. It occurs to me to ask her to stay with Lionel, but when I open my mouth, she shakes her head.

"He's long gone. Marcus' death will have driven him even further away," she assures me.

"How'd you know what I was going to ask?"

"Intuition. As hard as it is for you to believe, I have had close friends in my life."

We make our way to Cecily's house, which is only about ten minutes away. As we go, I decide to try to continue our conversation from earlier.

"So how long ago is 'back in your day'?" Lordy, I'm tactful.

"Do you also want to know how much I weigh and whether this is my natural hair color?" she replies. I put my hands up and leave her alone for the rest of the ride. She's still mad at me for the way I reacted to her inhumanness, I guess. In fact, she may never forgive me. Apparently she's only going to play nice around Lionel. I wonder if that's evidence that she likes him. I hope so, for his sake.

When we get to Cecily's, she leaves me to the dogs and goes upstairs. I assume I'm supposed to wait, so I sit on her couch and idly pet Sas, who's sitting in front of me. My eye is drawn to the old photograph of the two-toned hair guy. It's just so out of place among the full-colored photos around it, even if the guy looks modern.

Cecily comes back with a round mirror about the size of a dinner plate. It's the kind you buy in craft stores for the purpose of decorating them, but this one is completely unadorned. She places it carefully on her coffee table and pulls a simple chain bracelet out of her pocket. It pools gracefully onto the mirror's surface.

The sorcerer hops up and goes to the kitchen. Her dogs follow her this time. Probably hoping for some treats. I don't dare touch the mirror or chain, even though I'm dying of curiosity. Cecily's probably going slow on purpose to annoy me.

She comes back with a Rolodex card. When she sits next to me, I read the name at the top: Ceres Dixon. There's an address under the name, but instead of a phone number there's a curvy sigil.

"Seer-reez?" I try.

"Like the Roman goddess, yeah. But you'll call her Ms. Dixon unless she tells you otherwise."

"Noted."

Cecily focuses on the card for a second, and I see a subtle warping of the air around it before she places it on the mirror. The surface of the glass ripples like water for a few seconds before a blurry image appears in the air above it.

Ceres Dixon is a short, plump black woman with large, luminous brown eyes and her hair tied up in the most colorful scarf I've ever seen in my life. She's wearing another one around her shoulders under a huge gold pendant.

"Cec'ly! Love! I been wonderin' 'boutchu for quite some time," she drawls, grinning a very white grin. Sas sits back on his haunches, looking very confused by the floating window. He puts his ears back and whines at Cecily, who gently rubs his head and murmurs calming words. He rests his head on her lap and closes his eyes.

"Hey, Ceres. I've been pretty busy. This is Patrick... ?" Cecily stops and looks at me.

"Litten. Patrick Litten."

"He's a Slewfoot on official business," Cecily continues. Then she tells Ceres the whole story. The bescarfed lady is attentive, nodding and making affirming noises when necessary.

"Shoulda know ya'd on'y call me when ya needed somethin'," she says, but there's a hint of a smile around her full lips.

"Sorry."

"Naw, naw, I c'n see ya been crazy runnin' around with Slewfeets and witches." Ceres practically spat the word. I hadn't asked, but now I assume that Ceres is also a sorcerer of a kind, which denotes automatic aversion to witches.

"Ms. Dixon, can and will you help?" I ask, wanting to hurry this along. Despite Cecily's reassurances, I'm still worried about Lionel.

The diviner regards me for a long moment with her lips pursed. "Well, sugah, I dunno that ya c'n afford me 'n all."

"Ceres," Cecily admonishes gently. Ceres' mouth splits into another grin.

"I'm jus' messin' wit' 'im, Cec'ly! O' course I'll give it a go. And you, Patrick, you go on an' call me Ceres, ya hear?"

"Yes ma'am," I say. "Thank you."

"I'll be there in two wags o' a pup's tail, you mark me." She disappears from the window in the air, which fades away. Cecily picks up the mirror, balancing the chain and card on top of it, and puts it on the floor by the coffee table before padding off up the stairs again. The dogs follow her, Sas looking over his shoulder several times before he disappears from view.

Not ten seconds after she leaves, the air over the mirror opens up again with a shimmer. It gets pretty big, and then Ceres steps out of it lugging a large velvet bag that reminds me of representations of Santa's toy bag.

"Well, don'tcha jus' sit there, boy, gimme a hand," she gripes. I quickly get to my feet and take the bag from her. It's heavy and there's something clanking around inside it. Once I get it to the floor, I loan an arm to Ceres as she steps out into the house.

"S'ch a gentleman," she purrs, patting my arm. There's a lot of barking from the top of the stairs and Sas comes thundering down at top speed. I'm surprised he doesn't tumble head over heels. He vaults the last three steps and careens into the living room, heading straight for Ceres.

To my surprise, she kneels down and opens her arms. He barrels into her, licking her ears and pawing at her scarves. Clearly, they've met.

Cecily chooses that moment to come back into the room, and Ceres bustles over to her, smoothing her hair and giving her a bear hug. I can see that Cecily's surprised, but there's also a confusion on her face that I don't get. Maybe she's just not used to being hugged anymore.

"You don' look a day o'er three hunnerd, love," Ceres bubbles. Cecily manages a smile.

"You haven't changed a bit, either," she replies.

"Now, let's get on." Ceres is suddenly all business. "I got otha things t'do t'day."

Sas refuses to be left at home, so he gets into the backseat with Ceres. As we drive back over to Bryant's house, I start to feel nervous again. When we pull up, I can see that outside the house there are no signs of a struggle. All of the lights are on, too. Still, I keep my hand on my baton as we head up the porch stairs. Out of the corner of my eye, I see the air warping just a bit around Cecily's hand. Ceres hangs back and tries to keep her bag from clanking.

Lionel opens the door before we get to it.

"That was quick," he says, nodding to Ceres. "I am Lionel Swift."

"Ceres Dixon. My goodness, Cec'ly, you do keep yo'self some darlin' comp'ny."

Lionel blushes and bustles off into the house again. Ceres grins widely at Cecily and follows him.

"She likes to flirt, doesn't she?" I ask Cecily, who rolls her eyes and nods.

"She's a good lady," is all she says in response before going into the house. It occurs to me that if I'd been faster on the uptake, I might have told Cecily that she was a good lady, too. I guess I'm finally starting to realize that, as cold as Cecily can be, she isn't bad just because she's not human. There goes my worldview.

Lionel and Ceres are already in the attic. She's circling the Lookers, tut-tutting and patting the human.

"Poor thangs. I tell ya, witches." She shakes her head. "Tha's gotta be torture, lemme tell ya."

"Any ideas?" I ask her.

"Not 'til I get a look at what 'appened, love." Ceres opens up her bag and starts setting out the contents. Mostly I see a lot of candles and a piece of chalk.

"I'm not trying to be offensive, but I thought witches used rituals and sorcerers didn't," I say to Cecily.

"No, what I said was witches HAVE to and sorcerers don't. But this doesn't count because Ceres is a diviner, which is different from both. She just doesn't like witches because witches are terrible."

I sigh. "Right."

"Divining is learned magic, like witchcraft, but the learner still has to have innate psychic powers to use it. In fact, psychic abilities tend to drive their users mad if they *don't* learn how to focus it with divining," Cecily continues.

"You still teachin' them classes, ain't ya?" Ceres chuckles from her place on the floor next to the Lookers, where she's drawing a circle around herself. "I c'n tell by ya tone."

Cecily smiles a little. "Am I explaining it right?"

"Shit, girl, you been seein' all kinds o' stuff since way afore I was an idea, so if'n ya say something I think's wrong, I still ain't gonna contradict ya."

By now, Ceres is setting the candles up around the perimeter of the circle. There are tall tapers, little tealights, different colors, and even one big vanilla-scented candle in a glass container. I guess as long as it lights, it serves a purpose. I have my doubts when she pulls out a Christmas candle shaped like a peppermint, but Cecily seems unconcerned.

I know she drew a circle because I saw her do it, but by the time she's done setting up the candles, the line is completely gone. I wonder what the point of drawing it was. Oh well, I'm not the expert. Ceres lights every one with a long lighter while humming to herself. For a second, I tense up, expecting to feel some magic, but then I realize that she's humming "Amazing Grace." I glance sideways at Cecily, but the sorcerer just looks bored.

Lionel, on the other hand, looks utterly fascinated. He's counting the candles under his breath and keeps looking back and forth between Ceres and the Lookers like he thinks something's changing. He's actually studying the process. What a nerd.

After she's lit the candles, Ceres takes a few metal containers out of her bag. I'm guessing those are the source of the clanking. They're all different sizes and made of pewter or iron. She unscrews the top of the first one and pulls out a long white obelisk. I'm pretty surprised when she removes her scarf and sticks it down her shirt. The tip is peeking over her collar.

Once she's got her scarf situated again, she moves onto the next container. This one's full of black dust, which she sprinkles liberally over the top of her head. The third container, a flat circle, holds a spicy-smelling salve that she smears under her eyes.

"Heart, mind, 'n eyes," she tells Lionel when she sees him watching. "All gotta be enhanced."

She rubs her hands together as her face settles into a serious expression. "All righty. I'm gonna need mah space now, so y'all step back. I don' want ya ta leave th' room, since y'all know what you're lookin' for, but I don' want ya in the way neither."

We all obediently take a few steps back so that we're against the far wall. Ceres crosses her legs lotus-style and closes her eyes. Her body falls into a relaxed state. I expect some chanting or humming, but she stays silent. I can feel the tension in the air, lifting the little hairs on the back of my neck. Something's definitely happening.

Suddenly, the door to the attic slams open... no, wait, it's more like a ghost of it slammed open. I can just barely see the real door still closed, but a spectral light from the "hallway" below is shining through it. A slightly-transparent balding man climbs up. He looks scared. He's wearing an old sweater and dark khakis and has purplish circles under his eyes from exhaustion.

He stumbles to the far wall from us and spins around, but he no longer looks scared. He's got a manic grin on his face that reminds me uncomfortably of Marcus and I think I'm looking at Head. He's not as impressive as I thought he'd be.

That's when I glance down at the ground and see a sigil burned into the wood and a rodent skeleton laid out over it. I realize what happened before it does: the Lookers walked into a trap. As the two barge through the door, I wish I could call out to them. But as soon as the human one steps on the sigil, he hits the ground like a sack of potatoes and rolls onto his back, motionless. I hear the shattering of the rodent skeleton when he lands on it. The ghost Looker sort of trips over him, but instead of falling, his body jerks upward and he ends up in the position we can see him in now.

Head smirks and leaves without a word. I get a look at his face, round and weathered, and I shudder. The skin around his eyes has gone completely black and there's a yellow tint to his blue irises. The evil is almost palpable.

Cecily is standing close enough to me that I can feel her shaking. I assume with hatred and fury. As the image fades into the here and now, she moves away and shoves the human Looker over. I almost call out a warning, but she knows what's going on better than I do.

"Burned in with alder wood and painted over with a child's blood," Cecily says. "Plus there was the rat skeleton."

"So you are familiar with this, then?" Lionel asks as he squats next to her.

"Nasty magic," Ceres puts in, standing and stretching.

"It is. They're basically trapped in their own bodies." Cecily runs her finger over the edge of the sigil, frowning. "Fortunately, I think we can just destroy it. Too bad we were too freaked out to just turn him over before."

"Seriously? All that, and we can take care of it just by destroying a mark in wood?" I feel dumb.

"It will alert Head," Cecily admits.

"Do you think he would come back here?" Lionel sounds skeptical. "After all, he has seemed reluctant to face off against us until now."

"Actually, I was thinking it'd chase him further off and make him even harder to find. He'll know that all of his crimes have been discovered."

"Could you help us find him? We know some of the places he's been," I say to Ceres.

"Naw, hon. I seen that guy clear as you and I ain't gettin' in his way."

I immediately start feeling the same resentment for her that I did for Cecily before the big battle with Marcus. Is this refusal to stick your neck out a trend in the magic community? I open my mouth, but Lionel comes to my rescue.

"Our gratitude for your help, Ms. Dixon."

"Gratitude nothin', darlin'." Ceres eyes us shrewdly. "What do ya got for payment?"

I turn my glare on Cecily. She shrugs and pointedly goes back to the mark in the floor.

"We were, ah, under the impression that you came to our aid in a volunteer capacity," Lionel tries.

"Well, you were under the wrong impression, handsome. I don' do anythin' for free. 'Specially when I'm doin' somethin' might piss off major players. Cec'ly, love, ya should've mentioned my fee."

"Probably," is all Cecily says in response. I want to strangle her.

"Well. I see. Ah, how much do you require?" Lionel asks, resigned, as he pulls out our checkbook.

"I don' deal in money, hun. Cec'ly, ya really done dropped th' ball here," Ceres snaps. "How d'ya even know that they got somethin' I'd want, ya little brat?"

"They're Slewfeet, Ceres. Of course they've got something you want, or know something you want to know," Cecily argues without looking up. The air is warping around one of her hands, so I figure she's about to deal with the mark.

"And you'd better decide quick, because once Cecily hits the floor there, Head might come back," I add in a stroke of inspiration. Ceres turns her dark eyes on me, and while she tries to look severe, I see the flicker of fear.

"How 'bout an IOU?" she says finally. "But don'choo think for one little minute that I ain't comin' to collect."

"Okay." I shrug. Ceres nods curtly at Lionel and I, pats Cecily affectionately on the shoulder, and bustles off down the stairs. I hear Sas bark once, and then silence.

"Are we ready?" Cecily asks.

"Do you really think he's going to show up?" My hand goes to my baton.

"If he does, he's going to be pissed." Cecily doesn't sound nearly worried enough, but then, I've seen what she can do. Maybe I'm more worried than I should be.

"I think it best for us not to attempt engagement if he does appear," Lionel says. "He may have some very unpleasant and unpredictable tricks up his sleeve. Pardon, Cecily, but witches do seem to be a bit more, ah, varied in their skill sets than sorcerers."

I stare at him. "Did you just call her a one-trick pony?"

Lionel blushes, embarrassed. "I assume she understands my meaning. After all, she is still the most powerful and skilled creature I have ever--"

"I got it," she interjects.

"Right." Lionel's face gets redder.

"And he's not wrong," Cecily continues. "Head seems like the type to set things up in advance. It's a sure bet that he'll be ready for a fight if he comes back here. Best case scenario, I can get through his defenses and knock his brains out with a wall. Worst case: he kills me."

"Those two scenarios are pretty far apart on the spectrum," I say.

"My point is, if he shows up, there's going to be a fight. And it could go either way. Maybe you guys should just get clear."

"I'm getting pretty tired of being unable to help," I snap. "Isn't there something we can do against him?"

"I mean, you're welcome to shoot at him."

I blink. "Would that help?"

"Probably not, but it's worth a shot." She offers me a small smile, which is more than I'm used to seeing from her. "I can tell that you'd rather stay here, so I'm not going to make you leave."

She slams her palm into the mark. The section of floor, about the size of a large dinner plate, caves in due to the invisible force around her hand. The mark is no longer readable; it's fissured with cracks and mashed together.

"Probably could have just taken a knife to it, but this is more fun," Cecily says thoughtfully.

We wait. Lionel has his gun out and is ready to shoot at something even if he won't hit it. I've decided that my baton really would be my friend here, so I'm cradling it in my hands. Don't judge - it's my baby. Cecily hasn't moved from her spot on the floor, but her cat-slit eyes are moving around, trying to look in every direction at once.

A good twenty minutes later, there's still no sign of Head. The Lookers are just starting to blink and twitch, so Lionel kneels down to help them as much as he can.

"Sas will bark if anything happens," Cecily says. She comes up from her crouch with a wince.

"He could probably stand to go outside by now, right? I'll take him if you want," I offer. She nods, popping various joints, and I head down the stairs.

Sas lolls his tongue and wags his tail at me. Despite not being the biggest animal lover, I can't help but kneel down and give him a good scratch under his leonine ruff.

"No licking," I tell him as he moves forward. He backs up as though he can understand me, and instead puts a huge paw on my knee. Uncanny.

"Want to go outside?" I ask, patting his paw and then standing up. He bounds down the hallway ahead of me. When I don't walk fast enough, he comes back for me, circles my legs, and then takes off again. Maybe I should rethink my dog opinions, because it's pretty adorable.

He does his business once we get outside and then I let him sniff the strange yard for a few minutes. I use the opportunity to stretch out my arms and back. As I do, I happen to glance up.

That's when I spot the dark clouds rolling towards us on the horizon. They're not natural - I can tell because they're deep purple - and they're coming fast.

"Sas!" I call in a deep manly voice, not a little girl shriek at all. The dog looks up from his fascinating find, spots the clouds, and nearly falls over in his haste to get back to the house. He barks a lot louder than I can yell, so I give him the job of alerting Cecily and Lionel.

We tumble into the house. Cecily is standing in the living room. Her eyes are wide as she stares out the window. That's not a good sign: the extremely powerful sorcerer is afraid of what's coming.

I lock the door, though from the look on Cecily's face I don't think that's particularly helpful. Before I can do anything else, she blazes into action. Literally shoving me aside, she gets down on her knees in front of the door and starts chanting in a clipped, fast tone. She yanks the chain off of her neck, palming whatever's on it before I can see it, and spreads the length of gold along the bottom of the doorframe.

"Go into the bedroom and bring me those shoeboxes," she says. It doesn't even occur to me to question her; I trip over my own feet running for the room, but I don't fall. There are four shoeboxes that I balance semi-precariously on my arms as I hurry back to Cecily. She indicates that I should put them down and open them for her. Once that's done, she tears her eyes away from the doorframe and starts rooting around in them, chanting the whole time. I glance out the window and see that the clouds are almost on us.

"Got it." Cecily stands up, white-faced. The bottom of the doorframe is dusted with dried herbs and a line of chalk. I arch an eyebrow at it doubtfully.

"Threshold?"

She nods. "A temporary one."

"And it will keep that from getting in?"

"Hopefully?" Cecily shrugs, but I can tell by her face that she's not as nonchalant as she's pretending. "It should at least keep that from killing us."

"What is it?" I ask, afraid of the answer.

"It's a curse of total destruction. Nothing fancy, actually, but effective."

"A *curse of destruction* is *nothing fancy*?!"

"Calm down. Go get Lionel and your colleagues. I can shield all of us." She smiles at me, but it's more of a grimace.

I think she's bluffing to make me feel better, but I don't say that. Instead, I do as I'm told. The human Looker, Nelson I think, is just now waking up. Hancock is sort of sagging in a corner, looking tired. Which is weird, since I don't think ghosts sleep.

"Downstairs. Now. Move," I snap and gesture at the trapdoor. Lionel goes immediately, but the Lookers eye me like I've lost my mind. They can't speak, so I have to interpret that as "let us rest for two seconds, you asshole."

"Head's aimed a destruction spell at us, so if you don't go downstairs and get behind the pretty girl, you'll be vaporized," I add. They move.

I'm the last one in the foyer. Cecily is kneeling on the floor with her arms wrapped around Sas' neck; he's going completely ballistic with a roaring bark at the door. His ears are flat against his head and I can see the whites of his eyes. I do a doubletake when I see that he's got one paw sort of awkwardly wrapped around Cecily's thigh, like he's trying to pull her close.

I get down next to Lionel. He offers me a shaky smile.

"I do believe that this may be the most frightened I have ever been," he admits.

"What about when the witches almost blew up your organs?"

"At least that was a surprise, if an agonizingly painful one. The waiting is the worst, I think." Lionel shakes his head. "And Cecily is hardly certain that she can protect us entirely."

I don't know what to say. Anything like "it'll be okay" could turn out to be a lie. So I don't say anything. Nelson and Hancock are standing around Cecily. They look lost and a little scared. Hancock will disappear into... Heaven, Hell, Limbo, whatever... if Nelson dies. Judging by the fact that Hancock chose to become a Looker rather than move on to what comes after death, I wonder if he's afraid he'll end up downstairs.

Or maybe he just wanted to do some good in ways only Lookers could, I don't know. I think I'll ask him if we survive this.

Cecily looks up and gestures at my partner and me to come closer. The group of us huddle around her. Sas has stopped barking, but his eyes are still crazed. Cecily is gently rubbing his head and making shushing noises.

I look out the window. The roiling mass of bruised clouds are crawling across the treetops on the other side of the street. Where it touches the trees, clumps of blackened leaves and branches fall.

It's almost to the house. Cecily puts a hand on Sas' head and favors us all with a small smile.

"Hang on," is all she says before it hits.

Chapter Eleven

The miasma slams into the front of the house with a muffled, angry explosion of sound. The windows immediately go dark and start screaming in their frames, like they're trying to shatter and can't. Sas starts howling, which in the confines of the shield is completely deafening - I forgive him, though, considering the situation.

Cecily closes her eyes, but has no other reaction to the assault on the threshold. I feel bad that she's our only line of defense. I wish there was something I could do. Since I can't, though, I just offer her a reassuring smile when she opens her eyes. It's the first time that the cat-slit doesn't freak me out.

I don't know how long we kneel there. The spell of destruction raging against Cecily's threshold is like a rabid animal. It almost settles into a pattern, so when a window does blow out, I jump a figurative mile.

It sets off a chain reaction. The windows blow out one by one in a row. Since the screaming stops, so does Sas' howling, but that's the only good thing to come of it. The miasma lets out a new roar, one that sounds almost triumphant, and blasts through the threshold.

In a split second, Cecily throws a hand over her head. The air around her palm warps and ripples outward almost faster than I can see, coming down over us in a dome. The tips of my shoes rise a bit off the ground as the distortion slides under me to create a sphere. Cecily's afraid that if she doesn't cover us all over, the curse will get in.

It's on us. I can't see any of the others once the spell closes us in. I know, with perfect clarity, that I'm not dead in a horrible way only because of Cecily's shield. That air distortion is looking awfully thin right now, even if I've seen her throw tons of rock and steel with it.

A hand gropes at my trench coat and latches on - I assume it's Lionel, so I grab the arm attached to the hand and drag him to me. Even though the howling winds are outside of the sphere, it still feels like we're fighting through a heavy storm in here. We hold on to each other for dear life. I can't see the spell, but it's everywhere, roaring and shrieking and hissing like an insane cat. A large furry body bumps up against my legs, so I pull Sas to me as well. He buries his nose in my coat. I wonder where Cecily is.

That's when she screams. Long and loud - but the shield doesn't let up. Whatever's hurting her, she's not letting it stop her from protecting us. Sas whines loudly, but doesn't move. She must have sent him to me. I feel a twinge of guilt as I don't move to find her, but I think I'm more useful holding onto Lionel and Sas, especially if she sent them over here.

Cecily's screaming turns into a string of curse words, not all of them in English. She sounds angrier than hurt. I can hear someone speaking back through the miasma. A deep and booming voice rocks my bones and hits my eardrums too hard. I can't understand what it's saying, but I hear Cecily clearly.

"*I said come in here and **fight**, you fucking coward!*" she shouts.

And it ends.

The spell dissipates without so much as a by-your-leave. I blink and look around at everyone, gauging their states. It turns out that Lionel is in fact the one clutching me. His hair is all askew and his glasses are falling off. I doubt I look any neater. Hancock and Nelson are a foot away, huddled down but not touching. Sas is already climbing off of me and hurrying to Cecily.

Cecily looks fine, if a little windblown. Tired, of course, possibly more so than she did when was faced Marcus. She holds out her arms to Sas.

Her hands.

They're blackened like she's been burned. The flesh looks like it might crumble off. Like the leaves outside, when the curse touched them. Her hands don't fall off when she pets Sas, but I see the lines of pain around her mouth. The dog must sense it too, because he backs off and whines.

The spell had almost gotten through. She challenged Head because she knew she couldn't hold it anymore. She'd been able to think that clearly through what must have been excruciating pain.

What has Cecily Hawthorne been through in her long life to be able to do that?

Lionel gathers himself faster than I do, and he's the one that catches Cecily before she hits the floor.

"Cecily? Cecily!" He gently turns her over and rests her head on his lap. Her eyes are open but completely unfocused.

"I don't have any," she tells him. "No soapsuds."

I glance at Hancock and Nelson, who are staring around the house... well, what's left of it.

The front of the place is entirely gone, door, windows, wall and all. The porch, still mostly intact, is covered in what looks like soot and ash. It appears that once the spell got through there, though, it centered on us, because the rest of the walls are intact. The floor for about two feet around our group is black, and when I poke it, the wooden slats crumble under my finger to reveal burned-looking, chipped cement beneath.

"Patrick. Patrick, she's entirely delirious," Lionel says, reaching over and tugging at my sleeve. I look down at Cecily, and though she looks back, I can tell that she isn't seeing me.

I spit out a curse. "We have to get out of here before Head shows up."

"Shall we take her to the hospital?" Lionel asks.

"We can't. One look at those eyes and the doctor will be calling the cops."

"We certainly do not have the medical know-how to treat wounds such as these!"

"Let's go back to her house and see if she has a phone number for Ceres," I say, but Lionel is hearing none of it.

"That will take too much time! She is injured now!"

"Lionel, we don't have a choice."

"If I may," Hancock interrupts. His voice is clear enough, but there's a buzzing underneath his words that gets on my nerves even with three words. Then I realize that he's not actually saying anything: it's coming from the speakers on the blackened TV.

"Uh, sure," I manage to get out as the confusion ends.

"Your friend will heal on her own," Hancock says to Lionel first. "She is of the supernatural set."

The relief on Lionel's face makes me smile despite everything.

"As for Head, there is nowhere we can go that he can't find us. We may find that remaining here would be as good as anything, as we won't waste time trying to hide and can instead prepare."

It makes sense, except for one thing.

"Do you know how to prepare for someone like Head? Because, no offense, but if you do, you should have done it when he froze you upstairs like an ice sculpture," I point out. "So, basically, the only person who could prepare us is on the floor talking about cleaning."

Hancock glares at me, and the TV spits out a little static. I take that to mean that he's done talking. It was worth a shot for him, and some of it made sense. I nod at him in apology, my own mind running overtime.

And something miraculously clicks into place.

"What if we just made it simple?" I ask. Lionel frowns.

"What do you have in mind?"

I grin. "Police brutality."

***

There aren't a lot of places for me to hide, but I make do with crouching under the porch with my gun ready to go. I'm a little worried that the wooden planks above me are going to give way and fall on my head, but if they survived the destruction spell then surely they can survive someone stepping on them. Still, I'm ready to roll out if necessary.

I'm hoping that Head won't notice me. I'm assuming he uses the front door like a normal person. I mean, he's not a normal person, so he might fly in like a bat or appear in a whoosh of smoke. I don't know. I'm making do with what I have, since Cecily's still out of it. I guess I sort of overestimated how clearly she was thinking when she challenged Head, though I'm still hugely impressed by what she did. She bought us time.

Bought me time.

The fact was that as much as I love Lionel, this is not a fight he'll be any use in. This needs brawn. Nelson and Hancock are resting up in case they're needed. After all, Lookers aren't feared for no reason. But the two have been terribly weakened, so we can't rely on them.

A car pulls up in front of the house, and I scoot backwards a bit. It's Head. He looks... well, evil.

The black I saw around his eyes in the divining has dribbled out into the wrinkles on his cheeks and around his mouth, giving him a diseased look. His eyes are now entirely yellow. He's wearing a black turtleneck and black slacks, though they don't hide that he's pretty pudgy. If it weren't for the madness going on around his face, he'd be completely non-intimidating.

The weird eyes are fixed forward; he doesn't even glance down in my direction. I'm going to take that as a good sign. He seems pretty intent on Cecily, or at least on the group in the house. Probably planning to kill us all in one fell swoop.

Not if I can help it.

He goes inside without preamble, his steps a muted clomping over my head. Lionel and company are situated upstairs, so Head will have to look for them - which gives me a moment to sneak up on him. Hopefully, anyway.

I wait for him to get out of sight in the next room from the living room, though, because the porch might cave in and I don't want to alert him to my presence. It hits me just how ridiculous this whole plan is as I slowly creep out from under the porch and check for him.

"This is stupid," I mutter to myself. "He's going to squash me like a friggin' bug."

Hopeless. This whole thing is hopeless. If I attack Head, he'll roundhouse kick me into Hell and then kill the others. After everything I've been through and seen, I'm going to die abruptly trying to win a losing battle.

I shake my head. People are counting on me.

And just like that, the hopeless feeling dissipates like a fog. Weird. I shrug off the last of it and sneak into the house. The porch creaks predictably, but Head doesn't come storming out, so I think I timed this okay. Once I'm in the house, though, I don't know which way to go. Barely two minutes into this plan and I've already caught a snag.

Still, I'm on the clock now. I move forward.

No sign of Head by sight or sound. Where in the hell did he go? Maybe he needed to use the little witches' roo--

This is not going to work. I can't do this. I can't protect my friends. All I've got is brawn, no brains... brawn and a gun. What good is that against something like Head? I am completely useless in this fight. I should just run.

Whoa, what?

I frown and shake my head, but the thoughts keep coming. It's like my brain is telling me all these horrible things without me actually thinking them first. Like maybe they're not actually coming from me.

I hear footsteps and throw myself into the hallway off of the living room just before Head walks into the room. I'm not hidden from anyone looking in from outside, but Head can't see me. The onslaught of negative thoughts intensifies; I barely manage to keep my feet as depression sets in.

It's Head. Being around him makes this... miasma of negativity happen. I chance a glance around the doorframe. He's wearing a belt that has a few little trinkets clipped to it, and one of them is glowing with a sickening sort of gray light. I bet that's it. It's a spell.

As soon as I latch onto that thought, the rest goes away. The spell or whatever isn't even that powerful - I can just will it out of existence. It's just meant to cause hurt. It's a toy, like the magnifying glass a little boy would use to burn ants.

Head just likes dealing out sorrow.

My willpower is suddenly directed to keeping myself from letting out a growl. This guy just keeps getting better and better.

Head looks around for whatever set him off, but he doesn't see me. He snorts like an irritated bull and goes back into the kitchen. I wonder what he's looking for there? Herbs, probably. More supplies to make more spells.

He doesn't know Cecily is out of commission. If he did, he wouldn't bother to prepare for battle. The destruction spell must have taken up all the materials in his hidey hole.

I slip out of the hallway and tiptoe over to the kitchen door. If he comes out, I'm done for, but this might be my chance. I duck my head in long enough to see that he's indeed raiding the cabinets, and then I cock my gun.

He doesn't turn fast enough. I shoot him.

Except it doesn't hit him.

The bullet disintegrates into a fine mist about two feet from his head. He closes his creepy eyes and winces irritably as the heated dust hits his skin, but it just turns what isn't black into an angry red. I duck back, but he definitely knows where I am now.

My instincts scream at me and I hit the floor.

With a roar and scream of metal, a hole the size of a tire blows through the wall at about level with my chest. Pieces of shrapnel cut my hands as I throw them over my head and the back of my neck. When I look up, it takes me a second to realize that the hole is smoking, embers glowing at the edges.

Holy shit.

Well, glad I'm not underestimating this guy or anything. The hell was I thinking, trying to shoot him?

Instead of getting up and running, which he probably expects if he knows he missed, I skitter like a crab to the side. Sure enough, he fires again, this time scything the - well, it looks like a laser beam - from side to side and cutting the wall open across my chest level again. Everything, from posters to metal spars, is obliterated. The air smells sharply of molten metal.

I gulp. I am absolutely not the right man for this job, and that is not Head's spell talking. But I'm the only one who stands a chance.

So I skitter to the left of the doorway. When he comes out, I jump to my feet and hammer the butt of my gun right into his nose.

There's a terrific crunch and snap, blood everywhere, and a yowling scream that hurts my ears. I run for the hallway before Head can get the blood out of his eyes and past the pain.

Yeah, maybe I should have taken the shot. But if it doesn't work once, it might not again, and that would just be giving him time to man up. I run instead.

I manage to dive into the doorway and roll to the side about .2 seconds before another laser beam tears apart the wall. It would have missed me anyway, but no sense in taking chances. He's firing blind now, but he won't be blind in a second. That's when I lean around the door and fire at him again.

Again, the bullet hits some sort of shield and disintegrates. So it's specifically a bullet-stopping shield, since I was able to break his nose with pure physical force. That observation goes through my head in an instant, and I form some semblance of a plan. Not a great one, but a plan nonetheless.

I keep shooting.

Since his shield doesn't keep the teeny particles of metal from going through, he has to cover his eyes to keep them safe. Ergo, he can't be firing lasers at me. Well, he can, and he is, but I step into a seemingly random zigzag pattern and he can't aim since he can't see.

I get one step closer. And then another. It's slow going, but inexorable. And when my gun clicks empty, I pull out Lionel's and keep going.

"How DARE you!" Head roars with a much deeper voice than I expected. He touches something on his belt, and a wave of blue light explodes outwards in a ring around his waist. It washes over me, and I think, There it is. I'm dead.

Well, actually, I'm not, but I might as well be since Lionel's gun has stopped firing. In fact, it comes apart in my hands. So does mine - I feel it in my pocket. My cellphone breaks into little pieces. What's left of the TV sparks and tumbles off of its table. I hear the scream of metal as all of the appliances in the kitchen crash to the floor in a cluster of parts.

"It would not have occurred to me that you would use such a primitive object against me," Head says, finally getting a chance to wipe his eyes with his sleeves. His nose flops around a bit. "Otherwise I would have activated my disruptor spell before entering."

He smiles at me, and I see that all of his teeth are sludgy brown. "Live and learn."

"Brush and floss," I say, dropping what's left of the gun.

"Funny." He considers me for a long moment. "Now how to kill you?"

"I'm pretty easy to kill, honestly."

"I don't mean how, as in 'how on earth will I destroy this nigh-invincible obstacle?' I mean how, as in 'I have so very many options.'" He smiles again, reminding me of a shark.

I realize that I am, in fact, dead.

Chapter Twelve

I've got nothing. After a moment, Head lifts his hand, and a ring of some kind of black stone starts pulsing with blue veins. It's alive. Ick.

A sluglike tendril of bruised flesh and bulging veins oozes wetly out of the skin of his hand and drops to the floor. As I watch, frozen by disgust and fear, it twitches and writhes. I realize that it's growing. In less than a second, it goes from the size of a slug to the size of a small dog. Then to the size of a larger dog. It lurches and slithers towards me.

"I was saving this one for Hawthorne, but as she is apparently unavailable, it can have you for a snack."

The thing, now the size of a Rottweiler, lifts up one end of its chubby body. It has a smallish mouth ringed with dripping teeth. And not sharp ones, either. They look disturbingly human.

"That is seriously the nastiest thing I have ever seen," my mouth says without consulting my brain. The thing hisses.

"You'll hurt its feelings." Head chuckles. He sidesteps the thing and heads for the hallway. He's going upstairs to look for the others. I start to move, but the thing hisses again and wiggles closer to me. I bet it moves faster than it looks, too.

"Goodbye. You seemed a worthy opponent, but I've been wrong before," Head calls back to me without turning his head.

"Had you dead to rights for a minute there," I mutter under my breath. He doesn't hear me, but the thing does. With another bubbling hiss, it launches itself at me from its place on the floor.

I dive to the side, and it misses me by inches. Maybe not even that. I wasn't wrong about its speed, either, because I barely manage to roll over onto my back when I see it already flying through the air at me.

I'll never get out of the way in time. I just throw my arms over my face. I can still see the incoming mouth through a slit in my limbs.

A blur of black and gold slams into the thing midair and takes it down to the other side of the room.

I blink. My ears are being assaulted by a high-pitched keening and the sounds of tearing meat. I sit up and look over at the source of the cacophony.

Sas is tearing the thing apart as I watch. Translucent purple fluid is flying everywhere as it writhes and bucks, but it's dying faster than it can fight Sas off. Or at least, I thought that until it gets itself into a good position and slings its body around Sas' middle. Sas lets out a baying sound of pain as the thing begins to crush him. I guess it has a one-track mind, though, because it entirely forgot about me in the confusion.

I walk over and crush its head with my heel. Fluid splurts out and drenches my boot and pants leg; it's slimy and thick. Gross.

Sas wiggles out from under the limp tendril around his middle and shakes himself off. His big paws and muzzle are covered in viscous liquid, and he spits and sneezes for a second before wagging his tail at me. Despite the urgency of the situation, I can't help but give him a good scratching around his ears and ruff.

"Good boy. Good boy!" I praise him. He lolls his tongue at me happily. Together, we run for the stairs. The carpet muffles our footsteps, which is good.

Unlike Head, I know exactly where my friends are holed up. When Sas and I get to the second floor, I see the trapdoor down. He assumed they were in the attic, as I hoped he would. I grab Sas by the ruff and make him slow down - the hallway has a hardwood floor with a rug, and the big dog's nails will click if he doesn't go from the stairs to the carpet. I want to keep the element of surprise for as long as we can.

I wrap my arms around Sas and try to heave him onto the rug.

No dice. I can't even budge him. He even looks over his shoulder at me with a doggy expression that says "Are you out of your mind?"

I look at him for a long moment and try to figure out how to do this. Nothing comes to mind, and we're running out of time. I'll have to rely on that weird, uncanny ability Sas has to understand things.

I must be insane.

"Sas, this is crazy, but I need you to get on the rug without touching the hardwood," I say as softly as I can. He cocks his head. I close my eyes, defeated... and then he slips out of my arms.

With a wiggle of his rump, like a cat about to pounce, Sas crouches down and then leaps. He sails over the hardwood, and for a second, I think he's going to overshoot. But then he lands and promptly sits down to keep from sliding.

"No freaking way," I whisper to myself. He turns his head, lolling his tongue out again. Shaking my head, I jump across to join him, and we head for the bathroom.

Using his coat, Lionel has made up a sort of bed for Cecily in the bathtub. She's completely unconscious, and he's sitting on the rim of the tub looking concerned. Nelson's coat is on the floor and spread out so Sas can walk on it without making noise. I have to walk through Hancock to get in, and it feels like a million tiny shocks against my skin.

Lionel holds up a piece of paper. It says "So?"

I take the pencil from his proffered hand and write "No go" before handing it all back.

"Now what?" he writes.

I shrug. He frowns and adds "Must do something."

"Like what?"

Cecily lets out a little mewl in her sleep. It's the first time I've heard her sound like the cat her eyes make her resemble. Her hands look a little better - at least, there's no more blackened skin on Lionel's coat then there was when I left to hide under the porch. Sas trots to the bathtub and lays down with his chin on the rim, whimpering just softly enough to barely be audible. Poor guy.

We all twitch when we hear footsteps in the hallway, but Head passes the bathroom and heads into the bedroom. No one ever suspects that their target would be hiding in the toilet.

Nelson grabs the paper and writes haphazardly. "lionel is right can't just do nothing"

I have an idea, but no one's going to like it. I take the paper and write it down.

"We takes turns distract him, might use up items."

The color drains out of Lionel and Nelson's faces. Hancock just looks ill, which looks really strange on a ghost. I wonder if he pukes ectoplasm. Nasty.

"All Head power centered on items," I continue. "If we can make him use them up... "

Lionel takes the pencil from me. "He will be powerless."

"Already made him use one, don't know how many he has or how many uses in each," I write.

"It seems to be the only way," Lionel answers.

"can't we wake cec up?" Nelson asks.

"Hasn't she done enough?" I actually snarl a bit as I write. Nelson flinches.

"I vote that Nelson takes the first shot" Lionel is a little snarly too.

"Seconded" I write, staring hard at the human Looker.

"your going to kill me for her?"

"I will kill you for your horrendous grammar," Lionel writes feverishly, a look of horror on his face. Hancock, for his part, is shaking his head frantically. If Nelson dies, I'm pretty sure he does too.

"Sas and I already went" I point out "It's someone else's turn"

""I should be here if Cecily wakes up, as I imagine she would flatten any of you who tried to silence her before she woke fully" Lionel writes.

Nelson's face turns completely white, but he bites his lip. "ok"

"Just run out, be snarky, get out of way" I instruct Nelson. "Hopefully he'll shoot at you"

Nelson gives me a look that tells me exactly what he thinks of my "hopefully" and then heads silently for the door. Hancock bars his way, but after they have what looks like a mental conversation, Nelson walks through his partner and out the door. The rest of us hunker down and listen.

Long silence. And then... Nelson screams. I hear the crashing of destroyed wall and smell the telltale tang of slag. More silence. Then the scurrying of terrified feet. Nelson made it!

"Come back here, urchin," Head says from way too close. I hear another section of wall's destruction. "I've already taken care of you once. Clearly not permanently enough."

That makes me wonder something, and this I don't want to put aside.

"The spell he used before should have killed you?" I write to Hancock, who nods. "Which of you kept both alive?"

Hancock stares at me without blinking. It's eerie and disconcerting.

"You'd better go help Nelson" is all I write. Hancock disappears in a cloud of static. Lionel glances at what I wrote and frowns.

"What brought you to this assumption? Ceres nor Cecily said anything of the sort"

"Why Head keep them alive? No use for them. So trying to kill them and failed"

"And this was important, why?"

"Wanted to know what we've got"

"Lookers are that, Lookers. They are not soldiers." Lionel looks pained.

"Why are people so scared of them?"

"Because they see everything."

"And take you out if you mess up"

Lionel shakes his head. "Rumor."

I stare at him. I can feel the color draining from my face. "Oh shit"

"Right. We have nothing more than we did before we met Cecily."

"Great distractions then" I try, but Lionel shakes his head and turns back to the sleeping sorcerer. Sas looks at me, but as he's a dog, I can't read his expression. I think the battle must have gone downstairs because I can't hear anything except an occasional bang.

Sas licks Cecily's arm gently and then pads over to me. He points his nose at the door and then gives me a look.

I nod, and he pushes the door open and hops onto the carpet. Shaking my head, I pull the door closed.

"That dog" I write. Lionel nods, but his attention is still on Cecily. I try to distract him with more about Sas, but he barely glances at what I write. If I weren't already hoping Cecily will wake up for her own sake, I'd wish it purely for Lionel's. The guy's got it bad.

The banging gets more frequent. Sas must have jumped in - I can hear his furious barking in between spells firing off. I decide that I just can't sit here and do nothing anymore. Besides, a good general doesn't stay behind and let the troops do all the work, right?

I wave at Lionel and head out before he can stop me. Hopping from the bathroom to the carpet to the stairs, I waver at the top of the flight. Head is standing right there at the bottom and firing off spells from the step like he's bored. Was I wrong? Does he have an unlimited supply of power?

I think back to the way he acted with me and think, no. He's just arrogant. He's confident that he'll destroy Sas and the Lookers before he runs out of juice. And he is absolutely not worried that Lionel or I will come up behind him and finish him off.

That... really cheeses me off.

Without really thinking about it, I draw my baton out of my coat, take the stairs three at a time, and swing at the back of his head.

Now, see, if I'd thought about it, I wouldn't have tried it. The shield that had disintegrated my bullets is most likely still intact, and I don't know how extensive that protection is. But by the time I come back to myself, the baton is already on the downswing. I'm committed and pretty sure that I'm about to lose my baby, and probably my life.

So imagine my surprise when the wrought iron and silver just swing right on in and clock Head right on the... well, head.

I'm no fool. I follow him down and hit him again. My baby is a heavy thing, and it's pretty clear that he's not getting up any time soon, possibly ever. I'm still a little too rattled to make sure.

Nelson, though, beats me to it. He's staring at the area above Head's back, and after a second he winces.

"Is that it?" I ask him. He nods. Sas comes padding up to me. His tongue lolls out in a doggy smile. He paws my leg.

"You did good," I tell him, and he wuffs a bit before bounding up the stairs to get to his mama. The Lookers and I stand around awkwardly, watching the blood pool around Head's body and wondering how on earth we're going to explain this to police.

"Speaking of police," I say out loud, "Why haven't we seen any?"

"Apparently, Head cast out some sort of cloak when he delivered the destruction spell. It allowed him to attempt our murder without human interference." Lionel is coming down the stairs.

I eye him. "How do you know?"

"I assume, as he is now dead and I can hear sirens."

We clear out in a hurry. Nothing we can do about fingerprints and Sas' hair, but none of us are on file and Sas isn't the only dog with black or gold fur in town. The Lookers disappear before Lionel and I get a still-unconscious Cecily to our hotel. I have no idea where Nelson and Hancock are going, but I bet it's back to HQ.

We tuck Cecily into Lionel's bed. Her hands and arms are still patchily covered in black, dead skin, but there are shiny pink patches of new skin peeking out. It is completely disconcerting and I distract myself by ordering pizza and fetching beers. Sas follows me, probably hoping for a snack.

In typical dog fashion, he seems entirely nonplussed by the whole day and is just ready for some food.

Lionel calls Jameson and starts giving him the report. From the sound and length of the conversation, Jameson seems less than pleased with the whole thing. I wonder idly if anyone would notice my clubbing him with my baby. Hate that guy, and Head sort of reminded me of him. Well, and other people.

I shake my head before I can head down memory lane and check on Cecily. Her eyes are fluttering a little.

"Hey there," I say, leaning against the wall. She blinks at me. Sas jumps up on the bed and lays down beside her, resting his head on her leg.

"Ow," she says, but not about the dog.

"There's my answer to 'how are you feeling?'."

"Ow," she agrees.

"Need anything? Food? Beer?"

"Shower."

I glance at her arms. "Isn't that going to hurt?"

"Not by my standards." She sits up and yawns. I start to help her out of bed, but she waves me off. "I got it."

She disappears into the bathroom, giving Sas a kiss on the head first, just as Lionel comes into the room.

"She's showering," I say before he can ask.

"Good. I am pleased that she feels well enough." In fact, he looks insanely relieved, but I'll let him think that I buy "pleased."

"Are you feeling well?" he asks me. I blink.

"Uh, yeah. I'm a little bruised, but--"

"I mean, you did instigate a man's death today by your own hands, Patrick." Lionel's eyes are concerned.

It hasn't occurred to me to until just now that Head was a human, not a monster. Or at least not a monster in the literal sense. He'd sure never acted human.

"I shot people yesterday," I say, shrugging and taking a sip of beer.

"I would think that it would be quite different, firing upon them from a distance as opposed to bludgeoning them physically."

He's right. My hands tingle, remembering the feeling of the metal clasped in them and the give of flesh and skull. Shaking my head, I address a different but related issue.

"I'm curious as to why it worked at all, actually. When I shot at him, the bullets disintegrated before they hit him. He obviously had some kind of shield up--"

"It was probably specifically set up against bullets," Cecily interjects, coming out of the bathroom wearing a hotel-issue robe and toweling her hair off. The robe gaps in the front, offering me a slice of pale skin and a glitter of metal. I wrench my eyes away, not wanting to risk Lionel's wrath.

"Or maybe even iron," she continues, oblivious to my struggles. "The silver in your baton would have busted right through that."

"So he knew I'd be carrying a gun, but not a non-projectile weapon," I conclude.

"All he knew was what he'd observed or been told." She shrugs. It does interesting things to the front of her robe. I go over to the bed and pet Sas to avoid looking, but he only looks at me with baleful eyes that tell me I'm not fooling him.

"What'd Jameson say?" I ask Lionel.

"Only that he would have preferred a more timely and less messy resolution," Lionel replies.

I roll my eyes. "Is he going to clean it up?"

"He must, yes."

"So, what, you do the work and your client sends in a cleaning crew?" Cecily asks.

"Pretty much. He'll make sure that no evidence of us is found at the scene and stuff. It's in the contract."

Cecily eyes me. "So only rich and powerful people can hire Slewfeet?"

"Normally we don't get hired. We're sent. Having actual clients is rare," I tell her.

"So who does your cleanup when you don't have a client?"

"Headquarters sends someone in, but it's better if the client takes the expense... and the rap if something sneaks through."

She nods and goes to the bed, climbing up next to Sas and snuggling into his side. He rests his big head on her hip. He's still staring at me as though daring me to come closer. Obviously, he's the jealous type.

I leave Lionel to hang out with the pair and go into the living room. My baton is sitting on the coffee table. I haven't cleaned it yet. Not looking forward to getting the gore and brain matter out of the grooves.

My stomach does a slow roll at the thought. I've never looked at my baby like this before. Lionel was right - braining someone is entirely different from shooting them.

But as I stand there, trying to will myself to move forward, I see a scared college girl with a keepsake necklace on the floor of a dark, evil basement. I see a pair of redheaded twins, one dead and the other having to live with it. I see a nerdy guy and a stern girl who could have had lives. I see a frightened housewife. I see a pair of burned hands, a wrecked house. I see my partner writhing on the ground.

I pick up my baton and start to clean.

Made in United States
Orlando, FL
07 December 2022

25728541R00098